THE
PORTABLE HORRORS
OF C. J. BOW

Meghan,

Hope these horrors do it for you. Thanks!

By

C. J. Bow

Rend Reality Publishing

Cover art by Rooster Republic Press

BOOK ONE

OF THE SPIRIT

BOOK TWO

OF THE MIND

"I had worked hard for nearly two years, for the sole purpose of infusing life into an inanimate body. For this I had deprived myself of rest and health. I had desired it with an ardour that far exceeded moderation; but now that I had finished, the beauty of the dream had vanished, and breathless horror and disgust filled my heart"

- **Mary Shelley, Frankenstein**

BOOK ONE
OF THE SPIRIT

WE ARE ACID 77

There's something happening here

But what it is ain't exactly clear

There's a man with a gun over there

A telling me, I got to beware

    - "For What it's Worth" by Buffalo Springfield

The following occurred in the Midwest with summer in full-swing during an annual training performed by the United States Army. This is a legend that has been told time and time again. Each time the tale is told either new details emerge or becomes further fabricated. No matter the machination, the proof of the story remains to be seen. The sole undeniable fact is that the soldiers involved in this tale are still missing with families heartbroken and downtrodden. This is the story of team Acid 7-7.

"Guard training?" Specialist Brandon Grant asked. "What the hell does that even mean?"

Grant, a Geospatial Engineer in the United States Army Reserves, who in his ten years of service had zero experience guarding a perimeter. His cohort, Sergeant Felipe Negron, who was four years Grant's senior was green just the same. Their job in the military was valuable everywhere but here. Naturally, their role kept them out of duty rosters for performing such tasks. This annual training, a culmination of Army Reserve units from California to the New York Island, from the Redwood Forests to the Gulfstream Waters, was proving to be dreadful due to sheer unpreparedness of their unit. With no mission to perform, Grant and Negron were shuffled around and lazily dealt place to place like an arthritic card-slinger at a poker table.

"I don't know, Grant," his first line leader Sergeant Kelven Horne chirped. "What I do know is that Captain Kenny wants two of our soldiers to head up to Camp Pointe, check into the mayor cell, and complete 'guard training'." Horne used air quotes as he didn't understand what guard training was either. Sure, there is training for pulling guard duty. Even in hand-to-hand combat training there were lessons how to protect yourself or gain control in the guard position, but never in his fourteen years in the Army had Sergeant Horne heard of such a thing as guard training. However, the Captain called for it, so the order had to be carried out. Grant flipped out his camouflaged memo pad and scribbled down the notes:

Camp Pointe - Mayor Cell - Guard Training? - WTF?

The sun pulsed, pouring down thick rays as Grant and Negron trudged a mile-and-a-half west from Camp Parrot over to Camp Pointe. Their load bearing vests were sparsely covered with empty magazine and grenade and canteen pouches; all perfect for seating packs of cigarettes. On their heads were Kevlar helmets with pads fitted inside for comfort. Strapped to their backs were old M16 rifles, standard for non-combat military professions, affectionately referred to as the "dinosaurs" of military weapons due to the outdated nature of the weapon.

Along the way they chatted about the first few days of the exercise; how it had been the 'worst they'd ever seen' and how 'disorganized it was'. They continued maligning their command team for their lackluster exercise filled with more menial tasks than mission-oriented training. In the year it took to plan the exercise, Battalion emphasized how important it was to be "battle ready", meaning each unit would conduct their occupations out in the field, simulating deployment overseas, to increase their proficiency in their skills. So far, the only battle they were ready for was the fight for the last pack of smokes at the ramshackle trailer posing as a store in the field.

∞

They arrived at Camp Pointe with the sun beating their backs. Sweat pooled at their shoulders and soaked every thread of their undershirts. Camp pointe was a massive square of hard-packed gravel with large metal containers for storing military equipment. Evergreen trees lined all four sides with entry points in the front and rear of the Camp. Clumps of soldiers were casted throughout with some building tents, some manning entry points, others preparing food for evening chow, but most of them were fitted into designated smoking pits basking in the haze of their cigarette smoke. Grant's instructions were to go to the Mayor Cell, where the command teams established their operations. Grant flipped out his memo pad and looked at his shorthand notes. He made his first strike through:

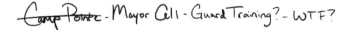

Camp Pointe - Mayor Cell - Guard Training? - WTF?

He had zero point of contact, no further instructions; just get there, look squared away, and tell them they were there for 'guard training'.

Grant and Negron pushed up the vinyl flap of the Mayor Cell tent. It was small and fan-less. Two junior enlisted soldiers sat at a desk with their uniform tops removed and twisted onto the backs of metal folding chairs in which they sat. One of the soldiers had a sleeve of tribal tattoos on his right arm while his left was bare. The other soldier wore thick-framed army issued glasses with fishbowls for lenses. Their attention couldn't be wrested from their cell phones. Yet Grant would try. "Excuse me," said Grant, "we're here for guard training?"

Tribal tattoo soldier peered dimly up to Grant and asked, "Gawd training?" His accent dripped from the east coast, which was thick and nearly impossible for Grant and Negron to comprehend

Fishbowl soldier joined into the confusion by placing his phone into his pocket and reciting the same last two words with the diction of a news reporter.

Grant scoffed and replied, "Yes. Guard training, where are they conducting the training?"

The two Mayor Cell soldiers connected eyes and sat there with mouths agape. Neither had heard anything of this training, so they turned to the radio and called their lieutenant to see what kind of training Captain Kenney was talking about. The call from the Lieutenant came through clear, unlike tribal tattoo soldier's indecipherable native tongue. His response was to send Grant and Negron to Staff Sergeant Benet who was gearing up for a roaming guard shift.

"So... where is this Staff Sergeant Benet then?" said Grant. The constant miscommunication was rattling his composure, yet he continued to breathe deeply and exhale sharply through his nostrils exercising some of the relaxation techniques he learned from some anger management class he went through a few years back. He took the class as a precautionary measure since he found himself easily agitated and often diffused his aggression with jabs of sarcasm which led to right hooks and uppercuts.

"Out that way," said Fishbowl soldier flicking his pointer finger towards the entry of the small, fan-less tent, then bent his finger into a hook implying further direction. Negron raised the vinyl flap to look and follow Fishbowl soldier's instruction. "Just look down that way and you'll see a line of generators, with hordes of soldiers just standing around doing nothing. I'm sure you'll see Benet down there, but he isn't very tall. So, it might not be that easy. And his temper isn't long either, so try not to piss him off, or tell too many jokes. He's about as dense as the 101 in evening traffic."

"What?" asked Grant. He followed everything he said outside of the trailing remark.

"You know, man. California. The 101. The highway. Hang ten and all that shit." Fishbowl mimicked his best surfer dude impression by raising his right hand with his pinky and thumb extending from a closed fist twisting back and forth.

"Oh, riiiiiiiiight," Grant lied still not getting Fishbowl's reference to the famous highway that stretches north and south in the three most west coast states of the lower 48. "Thanks for the disclaimer." Both Grant and Negron nodded in unison as they parted through the vinyl flap of the tent.

They grinded their boots into the dirt packed gravel down towards the line of generators, kicking up rocks all the way. At the very first generator was a short man hunched over a smaller generator unit. In front of him were maps of the surrounding terrain and various colors of pens spread out around the maps. Wrapped around his helmet was an olive-green band with two tiny glow-in-the-dark squares attached on the back, and on the thin band written in black marker the words SSG Benet were drawn. The pair had found their guy.

"Good afternoon Sergeant Benet, we're here for guard training."

"Guard training?" Benet said as his face twisted with confusion. He shoved the convoy route map aside which he was using to mark check points for the roaming guard for the night. He wasn't tall, marked as advertised. He stood about 63 inches on his tippy-toes, so to speak with Grant and Negron he jerked his head skyward to the two and continued, "No. I need you two for *guard duty.* We have an observation-listening post that we need bodies for. Besides, I don't even know what guard training means."

"Neither did we, Sergeant" Grant replied restraining his urge for sarcasm. "What are the hours you need us for this guard duty, Sergeant?"

"From now until Midnight," Benet said. He peeled the helmet from his head and used a sopped clay-brown rag to wipe away the sweat. Benet was bald with black and grey stubble sprouting from his temples wrapping around the lower bulb of the back of his skull. He swept the sides and back of his head with the dingy, brown rag, scratching against the grain like fine grit sandpaper.

"Midnight?" Grant asked, but knew he heard right. Benet nodded. Resisting the urge to roll his eyes, he continued "So yeah, our first line leader was under the impression this would be a block of instruction. I have to call 'em so they can determine what to do next."

Benet bobbled his head in agreement. He understood that these two were casted out for a detail without any information to be fed to the wolves so to speak. Grant phoned Horne and explained what that true definition of 'guard training' was 'a sideswiping bulk of bullshit'. Horne hemmed and hawed, then told Grant unfortunately his hands were tied, and they were stuck pulling this impromptu duty.

"Just be on standby," Benet instructed. "We got a few loose ends to tie up before we roll. Shit like comms hasn't been figured out yet so don't use up all your battery on your phones in case we need to get ahold of you, roger?" Benet said. His left eyelid sagged a little lower than the right giving the impression he was permanently stoned.

"Roger," they responded simultaneously with the enthusiasm of a teenager told to do their chores. Grant informed Benet they were heading over to the nearest smoke pit which was conveniently located in a shaded area where the grass was short and in view of Benet. Standby never meant what they wanted it to mean. Grant thought that maybe this time it meant ten to fifteen minutes at most. Negron gave Benet the benefit of the doubt with twenty minutes tops. Low and behold, they were planted in the shaded grass, burned eight cigarettes and sweat six ounces for two hours. At this point, the two soldiers didn't want to smoke another cigarette, but there was nothing else to do, and sleeping wasn't an option, so they lit another one.

∞

Like a cat blasted from a cannon Benet boomed, "Grant! Negron! Let's roll! You'll be riding with me in this Humvee!"

Scrambling to their feet and stubbing out their half-smoked cigarettes, Grant and Negron hollered, "Roger," and rushed over to the up-armored vehicle with a sense of purpose. Once they got inside Benet handed them each two magazines filled to the brim with blank rounds. They looked at each other and grinned knowing they weren't going to spend a single round. Cleaning weapons was not a well-developed skill for them, and the mess dead rounds create inside of the M16 after using them was a thorn in the side to clean. The vehicle popped and rumbled to a start and off they went to spend the next ten hours on a field 500 meters east of Camp Pointe.

When they arrived, Grant and Negron scouted their location. They took up residence in the shade of a tall oak tree surrounded by thick overgrown grass. Stomping the grass flat, they secured a favorable spot where they could lay down or crouch and go unnoticed. Benet threw out camo netting and poles to erect them to conceal them further from the 'enemy'.

The two soldiers tied the netting to the oak tree and stretched it out three feet each way. That was when Grant noticed something peculiar. On the tree, facing the field, a strange mask made of cornhusks was nailed to it. The nose was long and droopy, sagging beside an open mouth in the form of an 'O'. The cheeks high and prominent. The eyes bulged and leery, appearing to be looking up and outwards. A mane of straw bordered the mask. Perhaps the thing was a gag created by the bored soldiers who last manned the point, or maybe it was of some historical significance, placed there by the post commander to show their respect for the roots of the area, but no placard had been posted stating anything otherwise. No matter the reason, Grant was uneasy. An ominous and heavy presence emanated from the creepy mask. Besides, this place had clearly gone untouched for quite some time as evidenced by the long crawling, undisturbed grass. So, how could anyone had been out here and set this all up any time recently?

"You boys need anything else?" Benet asked as he reentered the vehicle.

"Yeah," said Grant. "Do we have any comms yet then, or..." He neglected to bring up the mask to Benet. Although strange, and off-putting, not pertinent to the mission.

"Well," Benet replied slightly agitated. "We're still working the comms angle, but just be on the lookout for suspicious activity."

"Like..." Negron interjected at the edge of annoyance.

"Look guys, it's the beginning of the exercise," Benet said. "There shouldn't be anything out here. You'll be out of sight, out of mind. Nobody really gives a shit that we're out here, but the battalion commander wanted some bodies out here, so there you go. Maybe it looks good on his quarterly review. Maybe he gets some sick joy out of watching soldiers suffer. Maybe he hates us. I don't know, but at this point it doesn't even matter. We're at the mercy of the Army Gods right now so the best thing we can do is embrace the suck and sit on our asses. Can you guys just do that for me?" Without bothering for an answer, Benet asked another question, "Anything else before we roll?"

"How 'bout chow?" Grant asked sincerely while shrugging his shoulders.

"That I can do," Benet replied with confidence. "We'll bring out hot chow when they open up shop. Fair?"

"Hooah," they both acknowledged in unison. Field chow was not fine dining, but it was hot, and hot food can cure a lot of woes. Pretty much anything was better than the ready-to-eat meals they were inhaling as of late. Something about the title of 'Pork-shaped Ribs' left a lot to be desired, and to think warming it up in the army-issued heat packets to get a better outcome would have been a lot like sliding cow pies into an oven and expecting quiche on the other end when you'd really just have a steaming hot pile of shit.

"Good. I'll see you guys in a couple hours. Hopefully we'll have comms up and ready for you two. In the meantime, jot my number down, just in case you need anything." He called out his digits as Grant jotted down the numbers in his pocket notebook. Above the numbers he scratched in *Staff Sergeant Shit for Brains*. His sarcasm was better suited in paper form rather than the backlash he would receive had he vented his frustrations through verbal micro-aggressions.

Once Benet and his driver took off Grant and Negron lit up another cigarette. The rays from the sun cascaded down harder than it had earlier in the day. It was the peak of Summer where reprieve only came in the shade or late in the evening. They took to the shade.

Camp Point - Mayor GH = Guard Training? - WTF?

"Fuckin' A man," Grant said as sweat draped his dark brown skin. "This is some bullshit."

"You ain't lyin' Primo," Negron agreed. His head bobbed as his cheeks caved, pulling smoke through the cigarette like a straw. It billowed out of his nose and mouth as he uttered his next words. "You see that mask over there?"

"Ah, yeah I did." Grant smiled. He worked his lips on the butt and dragged. "I was about to say something about that. Weird, huh?"

"Fuck yeah. I'm 'bout to tear that shit down. Lookin' at that makes skin crawl, you know?"

"Just leave it. Ain't hurtin' anybody to have it up there. Only your fragile mind."

Negron's eyes flashed at the insult, and let it pass, as he pulled another drag off the cigarette.

An hour elapsed, and another round of cigarettes were smoked. The sun had not relented. Grant downgraded his gear to his regular uniform top and patrol cap. Negron followed suit. Since they were 'Out of sight, out of mind' as Benet had said, they wanted to get comfortable. They unslung their weapons and laid them neatly under the concealment of camo netting.

A hawk's nest rested among the treetops to their immediate left. In synchronized fashion, three shot out, startling the two soldiers. They soared over the open field and presumably were hunting for dinner. After realizing what happened, Grant and Negron shook off the scare and laughed at each other, pointing out how they both flinched, and who was the bigger 'pussy'. They were distracted when one of the hawks broke away from the rotation and dive-bombed into the ground making an audible *thump* 50 meters south from their post.

"What the hell was that," Grant caught a streak of brown in his peripheral vision.

Negron was blind to the event, so he viewed Grant with a blank expression. He then watched him walk over to the area where the bird landed. "Que paso, Primo?"

"Hold one," Grant held up his index finger to his comrade while he proceeded to the landing site of the bird.

Negron heard a distant 'what the fuck' from Grant which piqued Negron's interest. He strolled over as his M-16 clanged against his back.

"I think it's dead," Grant responded.

"You think what's dead?" Negron asked, but answered his question by arriving at the splayed brown hawk. The bird's nerves twitched as it lay in a heap of feathers. They marveled at the mangled mess. The eyes were onyx black and the beak was touched golden bronze. All Negron could muster next was, "Damn."

"Musta been a kamikaze bird or some shit," Grant teased. "That's crazy, man. What the hell happened to a bird to make it want to kill himself? Had a bad day finding worms or what?"

"Nah, that's a bird of prey. They kill bigger shit like rats and coons."

"Excuse me?" Grant raised his eyebrow. "Coon?" Grant left a trace of race bait for Negron to take.

"*Raccoon.* Don't pull that shit on me, man," Negron laughed as he explained. "But for real though, that's a bad omen right there. Some weird shit going on," Negron began down a troubling trail of superstition.

"Man, get the hell out of here with your bad vibes and voodoo shit. Don't overthink it like you usually do Negron". Grant looked towards the tree line and saw another mask but said nothing to his compatriot for the simple sake of saving Negron's sanity. He knew that Negron would spiral out of control if he caught a glimpse of the long-nosed, shocked-face, eerie mask in more places than just of the one he knew.

Just then Benet and his driver pulled through the turnaround. "Hot Chow!" he said. The two rushed over thanking him. "What were you guys doing down there?" he asked as they approached.

"We were just checking something out, Sergeant," Grant replied huffing from the jog. He deflected by pretending birds diving into the ground was just business as usual. "It's nothing major. Just a dead bird"

"Like, freshly dead?" Benet questioned.

"Well, yeah," Grant replied. "It just dove from the sky right into the ground. No big deal."

"Weird," Benet said perceiving the two soldiers with a puzzled eye. The gaze lingered into an uncomfortable stare. He broke eye contact suddenly and resumed, "Anyway, we're going to hit the road again. We got some people procuring comms as we speak. Need anything else in the meantime?"

"I think we're good Sarge," Grant replied with a thumb up, and a mouthful of the Army's version of spaghetti and meat sauce. Negron nodded and remained silent with clenched jaws looking over to the area of bird remains. Benet hopped into the vehicle, waved off choking diesel fumes, and rolled away.

Negron couldn't eat while the mystery of the suicidal hawk hung in his head. He peeled off the sweat sodden patrol cap and scratched at the back of his bald head inventing whatever inane scenarios he could conjure. Maybe it was a witching thing. Or even satanic. He recalled horror movies where birds crashed into windows and it meant a demonic force was present. Or aliens. There was the one about the aliens too; something about a ton of magnetic force in the world pooling into a specific area, as a ground zero, where they were plotting world domination. His mind ran rampant with wild delusions, but none of it had a destination. Only a sole, lonely traveler down a path of pure lunacy.

Grant peered over his plate and watched Negron's scrunched-up face knowing his imagination was at work. "It was nothing Negron," Grant said shoveling another load of mixed vegetables into his mouth. "Just a dumb bird with suicidal tendencies. Now eat your food. You'll like it. It's awful," Grant joked. Apprehensive to dismiss all possible outcomes, Negron suppressed his superstition and moved on to eating his meal.

After their meal, they each drew out another cigarette and lit them. Negron's pull was long and relaxing. The buzz of the dead hawk slipped from his suspicious mind and his nerves eased with each drag.

Grant took a drag as well and drew his cell phone. 31 percent. "Look at that," exclaimed Grant as he showed Negron the amount of battery power remaining.

"Same," said Negron whose battery power was at 34 percent.

∞

A fox emerged from the tree line. He nosed the air and detected the scent of the dead bird. If he was a shy fox, it did not show. He glanced over to the soldiers, blinked, and continued tracking the scent as if to nod to the gentlemen and inquire the whereabouts of the dead bird. Not more than a few seconds did it take the fox to zero in on the carcass. He trotted over and circled the area hoping no other animal had sank their teeth into the delectable morsel. The fox advanced to the dead hawk only to sniff and prod it with his nose. It pedaled backwards and fiercely snarled training a steady gaze on the dead creature. With a sudden pivot, the fox turned towards the woods and bolted for the tree line.

Confusion flashed over the two soldiers. They wondered why the fox rejected an easy meal. "Bad omen, Primo," Negron reverted to his suspicious ways.

"Pssshhhh."

Benet and his driver rolled up just then and bubbled with excitement, "We got comms!" He stumbled out of the passenger-side door and grabbed a pack from the back seat with a large antenna sticking out of the top. The radio was clunky and cumbersome. Benet awkwardly slung the pack on his back and bounded over the tall grass where Grant and Negron were standing. With the finesse of a jackhammer, Benet slammed down the radio after it slipped off his shoulder in front of the large oak tree. Sweat splashed from his forehead and his cheeks were flushed red. Benet took a brief inventory of the pack and guided Grant and Negron through the contents of each pocket. Then, he explained how to change frequencies, how to begin a transmission with the handheld receiver, and a small laminated cheat card with the lists of call signs approved by the Tactical Operating Center, for Staff Sergeant Benet, the other vehicles on roving guard, and another call sign was highlighted. Lastly, he whipped out a radio etiquette cheat sheet, but Grant declined and reassured Benet he knew how to conduct a conversation via radio. "Have it your way," said Benet. For all the issues he had delivering the radio, he at least knew what he was doing when it came to communication systems.

"What's this one for Sergeant?" Grant asked Benet as he pointed to the highlighted line on the card.

"That's your call sign, Specialist," Benet answered.

"We are Acid 77? Sounds like a bad 70's metal band, don't it?" Grant smiled proudly at his comedic reach but once again Benet was not receptive.

"No," Benet replied dully. "It's Acid 7-7." He called off the numbers individually. "And no this isn't some terrible 70's metal band. This is the Army. So, you better recall those radio skills, that you say you have, before you have issues communicating with someone other than me."

If Grant's eyes could roll any further than they did he'd lose them behind his sockets. He knew better than to joke with a concrete mind, but it was a fair question. The 'Acid' call sign was unusual. The Army in general liked to keep to their phonetics, such as Alpha, Bravo, Charlie, all the way down to Zulu. "Roger," Grant begrudgingly complied.

"Sergeant," Negron asserted, "there was a fox out here, how are we supposed to protect ourselves? I'm thinkin' this place ain't safe."

Benet smirked, the first one to surface, and said, "You're in the woods, guys. There's gonna be wildlife out here." He took a moment to hoist his pants up then stand as tall as he could manage. "Besides I wouldn't worry about a fox. Far scarier things in these woods than a little ol' fox."

"Like what?" Grant posed the question with a blend of fear and intrigue coursing his mind.

By this time, Benet had made it back into his seat in the Humvee. He hung his arm outside the window opening and said, "I mean, there are some coyotes and snakes and bears, but we haven't seen anything yet. Probably won't. They hide from humans. Especially ones with guns. In the event it does happen, call range control and they'll walk you through protocol."

Negron wasn't satisfied with the answer, but he knew he'd create problems with Benet if he even had tempted to breathe a question. So, he nodded his head and said "Roger," in acknowledgement.

Like the last two times, Benet and his driver waved them goodbye and tore out of the turnaround to the main strip and continued their roving guard routes.

Negron looked over at Grant concerned. Nothing was sitting right with him. He could not pinpoint what it was, but a tingling sensation festered at the back of his neck telling him to trust his instincts and whatever was present was malevolent, and he was justified in his conspiracy deductions. Negron felt like this would take a lot of positive energy to quell the raging waters of superstition. In order to do so, he confided further in his companion. "Primo," he started, "I don't like what's happenin' right now. Bird diving from the sky? The fox acting all fucked up at some free food? I got this feeling something bad is going to happen to us, but I don't even know what. Like... I don't know. I feel like something... super-*normal* is going down right now. Know what I mean?"

Grant could not stifle his gut instinct. He gaped at Negron then broke out in heavy breaths and cackles, "He said... he said..." Grant did what he could to formulate words to articulate his amusement, but he struggled like a fat kid on a timed two-mile run. "He said... super-*normal!* A straight minute of babbling and guffaws followed until he gathered himself and asked, "You mean super-*natural?*"

"You know what I mean, man. I don't have to explain that shit to you," which was true. Those two were connected at the brain stem. Still, Negron blanched in embarrassment knowing that he had misspoke, but carried on firing back the only way he knew how, "Fuck you, man."

Grant collapsed, his back flat with the earth and basked in the joys of his friend's misnomer. He settled and said, "Nah man, there isn't any supernatural shit out here. A dead bird and a finicky fox ain't reason for suspicion. Besides, if there is an issue we can call 'range control'," he mimicked Benet's monotone voice and expressionless face.

∞

They crawled under the camo netting and took up a prone position as they looked across the field of tall grass. Conversation was minimal, and most of what was said for the next two hours was, "Fucking bugs!" They slapped at their head, necks, arms, thighs, and feet trying to ward away insect life. The heat searing sun had brought out the stench of ripe armpits and butt-cracks steeped in sweat. A bug's wet dream. Ants crawled all over their gear, on their pants zipping all the way up to their sleeves and some even breaching skin contact. Mosquitos came out in droves and rang in their ears with their infernal buzzing. Their location of trees and tall grass were cause for major concern of ticks. Since they were 'out of sight, out of mind' and in a meaningless exercise, they resorted to standing outside of the concealment of camo-netting, and smoked cigarettes instead.

Benet had been gone for over the hump of an hour when it happened again. Back in the sky, a trio of hawks wheeled in the still bright sky as if they were on a search party for their deceased comrade.

"I bet it's those same three birds from earlier."

"Same three? Do you hear yourself? Are you blind Negron? There is clearly a dead bird over there right now, so explain to me how the hell you figure that?"

Negron backpedaled, "Of course it's not the same exact three, but they are probably like the same family or something."

"You sound crazy. You need to take a nap or something, man. You're losing it. Your ugly face is showing it." Grant put it in the nicest way he knew how.

"Couldn't sleep if I wanted to, Primo. My nerves are shot."

24

Just as he completed his sentence, they both looked up and watched one hawk break off from the rotation. It swirled directly under the other two birds and torpedoed into the ground at breakneck speed, just as the first one had. The other two hawks vanished once the soldiers looked back up at the sky. Astonished, Grant looked at Negron, his neck canted off to the side. "That didn't just happen, right?"

"We should call them up on the radio, Primo," Negron began to sweat, but not from the heat. It was a different type of sweat. A chilling sort. The kind you get when something about your circumstance is amiss and you aren't sure if you should fear for your life or have a cigarette and wipe away your worries. Grant opted for the latter.

"What would we even say Negron?" Grant said with the unlit cigarette bouncing up and down between his lips. "'Umm Range Control, this is Acid 7-7, there are some birds out here with some serious self-esteem issues. They be dive-bombing into the ground to end their meaningless lives! There is at least three of them out here. Please send reinforcements. Save us!'" Grant coughed as he chuckled. He torched the tip and continued, "They'd laugh us off post, man, and I don't need that kind of drama in my life. Just forget it."

∞

Negron scanned the sky for the hawks. Like a festering germ in a petri dish, his mind was now preoccupied with the enigmatic behavior of the predatory birds to a degree which was burdensome. With what little battery power he had remaining on his cell, he scoured the internet to research birds mysteriously crashing into the ground in a centralized location. Instead of answers relating to his search, the search engines offered why birds crash into windows, or why they don't crash into each other in mid-flight. None of it was helpful. Then he researched magnetic forces, and what that does for animal activity. There he stumbled upon magneto-sensation and pored over the topic. It described how animals can track magnetic fields and use it as a guide while embarking on long travels. However, during his tireless search, nothing arose about animals all plunging into the earth in succession. His mind scaled with dissatisfaction. He stalked over to the most recent dead bird with grass crunching under every step. There were noticeable divots where the two birds fatally landed. Eye test landed them at about 25 meters from each other. Grabbing a compass from his grenade pouch, Negron shot an azimuth from the second to the first bird. The compass read zero degrees, true north, and not a degree off in either direction. He shuddered, looked over to Grant, and shouted the new information he discovered.

"Let it go, Negron," Grant returned, his back leaning on the large oak tree opposite the camo netting scrolling through his phone his legs kicked out and feet crossed. "Let. It. Go," he said under his breath.

He glanced back down at his phone. 23 percent. Grant began budgeting his cell phone usage to see how long he could stretch the life of the battery. If he intermittently shut off his mobile data and turned down the brightness on the screen he could manage until they at least were relieved from their post.

Shaking his head and trudging back, Negron cussed in Spanish and lamented his frustrations to the nature around him. 'How could he ignore something so un-fucking-usual,' Negron internalized on why Grant was so bullish to his speculation. Then, he recalled other times where the two had dissenting views; Grant with rationale and reason, and Negron with emotion and passion, and often Grant won out. This eased Negron's mind and he laughed as he approached Grant and planted his left hand on his shoulder, "This is really fucking me up, Primo".

"It's all good man," Grant reassured him, "don't get me wrong though. This shit is weird, but you gotta let it go. I've seen how these things play out in your head and it isn't pretty. Kinda like your face," Grant nudged him with his fist.

Negron broke into a smile and returned the action.

The western tree line doubled as a shield from the setting sun. Still bright, still hot, just less so. Benet's voice called over the radio, "Acid 7-7, this is Acid 1-9. Radio check, over".

Grant sprung over to the radio and picked up the receiver, "Acid 1-9, this is Acid 7-7," he paused lost in confusion on what to say next. "Copy. Roger. 10-4..." He winced knowing what he said was more trucker jargon than military protocol. A lump in his throat formed as he awaited Benet's response.

...

"That's a good copy, Acid 1-9 out," Benet disregarded the errant transmission.

Relieved, Grant sighed and hung up the receiver. He grabbed his pack of cigarettes and flipped the top. Three left. He thumbed the butts and shifted them around hoping to find a bonus cigarette, maybe even one or two that were partially smoked tucked under the ones crossed over. No matter how he counted them there was only three. Just like his cell phone he figured on rationing his portions to make it through the night. One now, the next one at the halfway point, and the last as a nightcap. Negron was drumming up a similar plan.

The sun shared shifts with the moon casting blasts of blushing pink and orange. Rose gold blended the two where they met. They both observed nature's beauty and discussed their futures after they get released from this pretend war exercise. Negron shared that he was

27

'going back to school for engineering', which he had tried and failed in the past on numerous occasions.

"At least you haven't given up yet man," said Grant. This was the perfect time for Grant to divulge Negron that his wife was pregnant. "Sooooooo... Stacy is with child."

"W-h-h-h-a-a-a-a-a-a-t-t-t-t?" Emotions flooded Negron as he profusely congratulated him and gripped him tight ratcheting him as close as humanly possible. Negron felt like his very own family was expanding beyond the confines of the traditional sense.

Everything halted when Grant peered up and noticed three hawks wheeling in the sky. "Shut. The. Fuck. Up." The words flopped from his lips as he started blindly reaching for the receiver on the radio. He groped the pockets of the bag, his eyes never leaving the situation above, attempting to draw out the card with all the call signs, specifically for range control, but with no luck. "Where is that card?" He asked Negron.

No response from Negron as he gripped the barrel of the rifle slung across his back. His mind filled to the brim with the endless outcomes. The alien invasion became more and more real. His imagination churned out lucid spaceships, shooting in from all directions. First zooming in with the rapidity of immeasurable speed, then halting into view - hovering above like when opposing sides of the magnets meet. Beams shot out from every hull, creating a thick, pulsing lines of light from each one with a mounting intensity which then blinded the entire sky. In a blink, both lights and ships were gone. Then came tall and stalky red demons with long, smooth tails equipped with veiny, fleshy wings which ambled from the wood lines. They closed in on the dead hawks where they leapt into the air and poofed into particles in mid-jump. Large ghostly hands of ashen gray and streaking white raised out from the tall grass. They knuckled up and slammed their fists into the ground sending an imaginary shockwave only to Negron. He flinched, almost tumbling to the ground, but only stumbled. His eyes never leaving the field.

"Negron, the card!" Grant pitched, his eyes growing larger and his mouth drier. "The one with the call signs? Where the fuck is it?"

Still seized by shock, Negron was rooted to the field and stood as still and unwavering as the large oak tree beside him.

"Jesus Christ," Grant trailed off and cussed, muttering any obscenity he could mumble. He dug back into the pockets of the bag in which the radio was located. There were three flaps and after searching the first two, he found the card in the third pocket. He went down line by line, dragging his finger down, looking for the range control call sign. Romeo Charlie 0-9. "Romeo Charlie 0-9, this is Acid 7-7".

Garbled static shot through the speaker.

"I say again," Grant burst with urgency, "Romeo Charlie 0-9, this is Acid 7-7"

"Look," Negron said mechanically clutching his weapon's sling in one hand and with the other he traced the hawk rotation with his index finger.

"Can't you see I'm busy man?" Grant barked as he briefly glanced at the sky. Once again, like the ones before it, another brown feathered hawk broke the rotation and drilled into the ground exploding into brown-feathered shrapnel. Grant blew his composure and raged into the receiver, "Range control, this is Acid 7-7, there are some Goddamn hawks out here doing some weird shit – diving into the ground and killing themselves – requesting some sort of procedure or what else we should do?"

The radio shared nothing but a silent, rhythmic wave of static.

Grant panicked and called to Benet, "Acid 1-9, this is Acid 7-7, can you hear me, over?" The radio boomed with crackles, stabbing his eardrums. Grant hammered the receiver down on the radio repeatedly;

his knuckles scraped against the metal, but Grant's adrenaline stowed away the pain.

He had been so encumbered by the radio that he completely lost track of Negron who was already half-way to the fresh dead bird. He shouted into the empty receiver, "Can anyone hear me on this goddamned thing?"

Grant watched as Negron had already made his way down to the growing graveyard. "Negron, what the ffff-ahhhhh!" Grant wrangled his swear word and attempted a quick mind frame restructure. His temper had already flared, but without providing oxygen for the flames in his anger he could reel in his composure. Grant plunged his hand into his pocket and withdrew his cell phone. 16 percent. He called Benet.

"This is Staff Sergeant Benet."

Thrilled with the sound of a common voice, Grant blurted rapidly "Thank God! Sergeant Benet, this is Specialist Grant, what's going on with the comms?" Grant had hardly come up for air, yet he dived right back into it, "It's-like-there's-a-white-noise-machine-on-steroids-bouncing-around-the-goddamn-radio-I've-tried-to-call-range-control-but-I-got-nothing-but-static-in-my-goddamn-ear-and-then-I-tried-calling-you-but-once-again-nothing-but the-fucking-loud-ass-noise-and..."

"Whoa whoa whoa – *Whoa*! Slow down," Benet broke in forcefully. "Now, what was that?" Grant reiterated his string of words but took time to breathe this go 'round. Benet returned with, "I haven't heard anything on the radio for the past half an hour. Try it again, this time with me on the phone."

"Okay," Grant scrambled to the radio and engaged the receiver. "Acid 1-9, this is Acid 7-7. Radio check over," as he transmitted his message, he could hear the echo of his call on the other side of the phone.

"Loud and clear Acid 7-7," Benet said.

Grant swallowed hard. "Of course, it works now."

"What's going on anyway?"

"The birds sarge. They're back. And another one just plummeted from the sky and bombing the ground like they're nuking the goddamn place. That's three now. What are we supposed to do?"

Benet worked at his lips. He had nothing. Grant could hear his mouth smacking over the phone, "Three? I thought there was only one. Now there's three? Yeah that is weird. Call range control."

"Roger," Grant said as he hung up.

Without delay Grant went back to the radio and called for range control. An immediate response! Grant stayed consistent with Army language while detailing the events clearly and concisely. Range control agreed the events were wildly enigmatic and out of the norm but assured him that the hawks would not attack humans unless provoked. Also, they informed Grant there wasn't a thing they could do to assist them. 'Only to stay covered under the camo netting and remain calm.' Grant ended the transmission with, "Roger. Acid 7-7 out".

By the time he tucked the receiver away, Negron was back. "Forty-five, one-thirty-five, forty-five, one-thirty-five," he muttered feverishly under his breath. Pacing back and forth at a rapid speed while slamming his head with open hands he obsessed over the numbers, "forty-five, one-thirty-five, forty-five, one-thirty-five."

"Neg.. Negron," Grant grasped at him while he attempted to get his attention. "Calm down man, Range Control said the hawks would never attack humans unless they're provoked. They thought it was weird too, but the only thing we can really do is just take cover and let the suicide party go down." Grant paused for a moment. "Negron? Are you even listening to me? Negron! Escúchame, you fucken prick! I need you here with me." Grant was losing his patience and mind all at the same time. He was afraid, but he needed Negron to come back to earth and ground him. That was not going to happen.

"*Forty-five, one-thirty-five,*" Negron said amplified this time. His frantic pace pushed Grant to the brink of straight-jacket confinement. He walked up to the tree and ripped the mask off the nail that had been pounded in between the deep groves of the tree bark. He cracked it in half over his knee and tossed them aside in equally opposite directions.

"Negron, *shut the fuck up!*" Grant erupted with spittle splashing from his lips. Embattled by the responsibilities of radio, bewildered friend, and maintaining the balance of sanity in his own head, Grant reached the peak of agitation. He let a moment pass and his blood dialed back from a boil to a simmer as he mustered with a low growl the question that materialized in his maw, "What the fuck are you talking about?"

"Primo, it's a perfect triangle," Negron gesticulated with thrusting arms over at the trio of dead hawks south of their post. "From the third dead bird," snapping out of a monster mash, he pointed precisely at the most recently fallen bird, then motioned towards the first dead bird, "Azimuth shoots 45 degrees". He then gestures over to the second dead bird, "Azimuth shoots 135. Don't you get what that means?"

"You're not as dumb as you look?" Grant said with his brow furrowed, less joking this time than anytime, and remained trained on Negron's eyes. He had his attention and hoped Negron would start making some sense.

"Listen, bitch," even with the setting sun easing on the heat index, the temperature of Negron's tone rose, "this isn't a game. Some super-NATURAL shit is going on. It's impossible. I don't know if it's aliens or demons or witches or whatever, but it's somethin', Primo. Would you just stop and think about that? For one time don't you think I just might be right? Just this one time? And that Goddamn mask is fucking evil! I seen them all along the tree line when I came back here. Don't act like you didn't fucking see them."

Grant shook his head, lying about his awareness of the masks. He shrugged at the rest of what he said. "All we can do is take cover under the camo netting, so they don't swoop down on us," Grant sighed as he tried to relax. "And all that other stuff you talkin' 'bout, I don't know. I'm not going to speculate or contemplate it, but what I *do* know is I'm gonna take a piss and smoke a cigarette really quick before we get under this netting and stay away from them crazy ass birds."

Negron stewed. He watched Grant as he walked away. He pumped his fists and clenched his jaws. His eyes darted back and forth from the dead birds to the back of Grant's head. Every impulse he evaded toyed with the notion of running far away from this field, knowing he couldn't run off without his comrade keeping him shackled to the large oak tree.

Grant lumbered down the hill to the tree line. At least out here he didn't have to jump into one of the poorly maintained Port-a-johns scattered throughout Army training sites everywhere. He could wet the grass the way nature intended.

Overwhelmed and stretched thin, Grant was ready for the day to end. While relieving himself, rapid winds picked up, jerking him back and forth before he could finally finish. "Ho-oly shit," he said as wave after wave of wind disturbed his balance. However, nature couldn't halt his urge to smoke. With his back still turned to the abrasive winds, he drew out his pack and flipped the top. Three cigarettes. "What?" audible only to himself with the wind thrashing all around. That's how many cigarettes he had the last time he checked, but distinctly recalled counting it and mapped out how he was going to smoke them. Had he somehow ended up with Negron's pack? Impossible. Grant had not bummed a single smoke from him during this whole exercise. Then, he questioned if he had even smoked that third cigarette when he counted them off in the first place, but he was adamant that he had.

That's when he heard it. Negron's strident cries piercing through the tempest winds. Grant's heart sank as he dashed up the hill. He couldn't peer over the hump to see what was transpiring. The loud screams from Negron cut through the savage earth and rankled deep in Grant's ears. His thighs strained as his muscles fatigued, still he charged with each step gaining difficulty. The breath of the wild halted all progress, causing Grant to falter, eventually sweeping his legs splaying him out in a prone position on the incline. He then dug into the ground with his fingers, gripping the earth beneath him to maintain his position. Each knuckle bent in ways he never knew they could.

Negron's screams turned to agonizing shrills. Grant gritted his teeth, his ribs a mixing bowl and his heart an egg getting beat to hell for a breakfast being cooked and served on a cold, dirty plate. His brain racked with panic and concern for his friend and knew he could not simply give up. Slowly, he churned his body and crawled, twisting up the hill, keeping his head low and his ear pressed to the ground. Nearing the top, Grant had finally worked up the courage to say something but was stopped short by the ceasing winds. The air was still. The screams were gone.

Grant rushed to his feet, stumbling up the hill. "Negron," he cried with exhausted breath. His heart wrenched tight, calling out for his friend, "Negron... *Negron!*" His voice filled the vacant skies, nothing but echoes reverberated across the field. The reeds gently swayed through the grass, but the wind had very much dissipated. He scanned the field, running around, and continued to call out for his friend, but in vain. Not a soul was listening.

Wasting no more time, he zipped over to the radio. "Acid 1-9, this is Acid 7-7. Over," He sped through the transmission with words tripping over each other.

"Acid 7-7, this is Acid 1-9. Copy, over". Sergeant Benet's voice crackled through the receiver. Static was mounting.

"Acid 1-9, Negron is missing. I don't know where he went. I went to piss and the wind started going ape shit and I heard him screaming, so I started running up the hill, but I couldn't, because the wind was too strong, so I started crawling, and he kept screaming, but then the wind stopped, and then he stopped screaming, and then..." static filled the receiver. His panic-stricken heart was dripping with anxiety. Swirls of wind brushed up against his skin and a tumbled mess of nerves shot through his body.

The transmission came in garbled, "Acid 7-7, can... say... you... cut...out... over?"

"Acid 1-9, can you hear me?" Grant called, but it was useless. "Can you hear me? Can you *fucking* hear me?" Feedback spiked through his eardrums and he winced in pain. Static took over. He threw the receiver against the large oak tree. It shattered into plastic shrapnel, shooting this way and that. Then he noticed a splotch of crimson on the radio. Smears of blood in the motion of a falling, pressing hand stained the tree. From there a noticeable blood trail had been formed through a newly trampled path of grass.

This drew Grant's eyes down the path and his gaze drifted upwards into the darkening sky. Three hawks spinning. Fear housed him, not bothering to chew while it swallowed him whole. He stood there, his mouth agape and his hands wrapped tightly around his face. His legs were chained to the ground, refusing to move even by sheer instinct. The howling winds returned and space all around Grant thickened in a shade of gunmetal gray. The remaining light in the sky

35

was blotted out by a maelstrom of hawks. At first there had been three. Then it was ten. Then twenty-five, then fifty, until they became a coarse innumerable line. He could not tell where one began and the other ended, all he could tell was that more were flying in, one-by-one, from all directions, adding to the seemingly infinite mass.

Terror held a firm grasp on Grant. He watched the hawks converge entirely and spiral like a spinning drill into the ground as the singular hawks had done before, this time landing eastward of the dead birds. Still, the winds raged, and the shockwave from the impact rippled through the field, ripping reeds from the ground, flattening the wiry, sprawling grass, and sent Grant tumbling back into the camo netting.

Wrapped up in the camouflage concealment like minnows in a fisher's net, Grant thrashed his arms and legs desperately attempting to get loose but getting more stuck all the time. Anytime now he expected to be screaming like his friend had not too long ago. The merciless wind blew like limitless lungs causing the netting to flap, relentlessly slapping his face with the sting of a whip at each crack.

He rolled on the bed of flattened grass until he could wiggle an arm free. With it, he ripped the netting from his other extremities and stumbled to his feet. That's when he looked up. The landing site, where the crashing birds littered the plain. A spire of brown feathers and clumped bird bodies were barely lit by the fading sun, rising high enough to force Grant to raise his eye-level. There they all laid lifeless. Some with their wings intermittently lifted by the strong winds. Others with their heads twisted all the way around. All dead. Except one. Perched at the peak with its eyes drawn taut to Grant.

Unnerved by the eerie hawk, Grant stared back with his jaws clenched tight. This hawk did not waver in the fierce winds. Instead, the hawk's eyes seemingly traced the outline of Grant, blinked once resetting its eyes squarely on him. The wings shot out from his sides while it looked to the sky, it's brown-feathered chest puffed out in pride. Defying all logic of physics, he gravitated above the pile without pumping his wings once. Hitting its apex, he stretched his wings even further, like he had been crucified. The sky was a deep plum now, yet Grant could etch every detail of this fearful creature in his disturbed mind. From its beady black eyes, razor sharp beak, expansive brown wings, long curled talons. Out from his pocket came the note pad he had been taken notes on earlier in the day. With a single stroke of his pen, he crossed off the final item on his list:

~~Camp Point - Mayor Cox = Guard Training?~~ ~~WTF?~~

The wind died, just as fast as it had picked up before. All was silent, and nothing moved. Grant even tried looking around, yet only his eyes would shift, and he would swear it that he could see time standing still. A blinding light split the dark night, searing Grant's vision sending him reeling in pain. He smashed his palms into his burning eyes and rocked back and forth to relieve the pain from the blast. Shock set in. \ His heart galloped. He opened his eyes. Surprisingly able to see, but not clearly. Black spots blotted his vision from when the pain pulsed through his orbs cinching his eyelids tight. His gaze darted up, down, left, right, and then he centered back to where the heap of birds was, but they weren't there anymore. Emotions flared from each side of the spectrum, elation and terror. Was he free? Whatever grabbed Negron, was it gone? Could he settle down and smoke a cigarette to calm his nerves. He would find out soon that he was not. Absolutely not.

Suddenly, a wide spire burst from the flattened grass in front of him, shoving earth to the sides. Broad wings shot out extended with shadowed arms stretching out to the sky. At the end of each finger were shiny talons. Above the silhouette the claws raised with wrists canted outwards under the radiating moon like a showing of praise. The head streamed with outward jutting feathers much like a native headdress.

Grant knew it wasn't human, and he knew it wasn't a hawk either. Everything he could see, touch, smell, hear, and taste were flushed out and replaced with an implacable terror his body was not fit to handle. He shit himself. It oozed down his leg, gently packing the pant leg of his fatigues. He tried to run, but his body responded with the speed of which one has when dreaming, exerting every ounce of energy yet coming up as not enough. As he spun around and took off, the shadow creature shrieked, the pitch loud enough to collapse buildings and crumble mountains. The shrill of the beast exploded Grant's eardrums, crippling him, crumpled him to the ground paralyzed by pain. His ears were hollow hallways now, only able to detect faint echoes of the explosion of his dearly departed eardrums. He clasped his ears like he could fix them, but to his dismay, they were just as useless as his attempt to run away.

He tried to get up, but the hawk-man-beast slammed into his back, its talons sinking into his skin with the ease of a knife slicing melted butter. Grant's ribs crunched under the pressure, bones tearing through skin and puncturing organs. He went limp. His fight was over before it began. A primal shriek ripped through the darkened clouds, and the creature shot into the now black sky with Grant laying lifeless in its grasp.

As the creature drifted skyward and into the all-encompassing blackened sky, becoming out of sight, out of mind, Benet and his driver tore into the turnaround, leapt out of the truck, and searched for the two soldiers, calling out their names in vain. They found load bearing vests on opposite sides of the oak tree, both weapons crossed up behind the tangled mess of camouflage netting, the radio system with smears of blood streaking across it and the shattered receiver, and the grass fortified in the blood of the missing soldiers.

∞

The Forward Operating Base mayor called all the soldiers of Camp Pointe to perform a police call in the field of long grass and then spanning into the tree line. When they found nothing, they called the mayors of surrounding bases to get a head count on their personnel and comb through fields to see if there was a trace anywhere. When that failed, the entire training operation, police officers, fire fighters, and civilians gathered and swept the entire city. All remained fruitless, as the only greatest source of evidence and information remained on that very field where it all occurred.

Rumors spread like wildfire. Conspiracy theorists littered the nation with fanciful and creative stories. Search engines were worn from the tireless use of speculators everywhere. Eventually, scholars and theorists delved into the event and dug up some worthwhile information. In their research they found that Native Americans thrived in that region of Wisconsin. Although the tribes that inhabited the area varied throughout the centuries of their prominence, one legend stood out highest above all. Retribution of the Thunderbird.

In short, the Thunderbird clans were a group of people whose jurisdiction covered all goings on from tree tops up to the blue sky. Their respect and loyalty to the raptor bird-family paralleled that of a Christian's devotion to Jesus Christ. One day, a group of five English settlers stumbled onto a plot of land, inhabited by four Thunderbird clansmen, while they were out hunting small game, rabbits, squirrels, and raccoons. Tempers flared from the disconnect in communication. The English readied their muskets and postured defensively, while the Thunderbird clansmen gripped their tomahawks and spears with white knuckles. What ensued next was a slaughter which left three members of the Thunderbird clan dead, and the English settlers badly injured, even maimed, but all alive. They retreated to their respective camps, while the sole Thunderbird clansmen survivor hopped on his horse to inform tribal leaders.

That evening, the tribal chief, the usual peacekeeper, was consumed by rage and sought to avenge the fallen clansmen by destroying the wrongful English settlers and devastating any and everything they held dear. He called on the spirits of the land to join forces and spoke more urgently to the birds of prey. Brown feathered hawks streamed from the sky and dove into the gravesite of the fallen clansmen. From there a Supreme Being stood tall with wide wings, massive talons, a feather-crowned headdress, and a body as black as shadows.

The Supreme Being tracked the English settlers' scent and ravaged their camp, killing all 32 settlers there. Swiftly, he disposed of the women and children by broad wing strokes putting them to rest with ease. The men that drew up their weapons and fired upon the beast suffered a worser fate. It boomed with a shriek and incapacitated all remaining settlers, all men with weapons drawn, now fight-less, which made the rest easy. One by one, the Supreme Being plucked up the remaining armed settlers, with talons sinking into whatever was available to him, and drew them up in the sky where he began to harvest on them. The blood, borne from the sky, casted like scattered showers covering every tent top and snuffed out every fire.

After the massacre subsided and the blood crusted over the land, the chief was stricken with guilt. His remorse plagued him, splintering his soul which then spread like an aggressive cancer amongst the clan. He wanted to undo what had been done, but it was too late. No amount of sorry, or praise, or offering would give back the life of the expired English settlers. This war of conscience weighed heavy on his chest and would not rest until this creation of evil was deconstructed. The problem was that the Supreme Being could not be destroyed. However, it could be confined. Tribal leaders of the surrounding area, including the sole Thunderbird clansmen survivor, gathered upon a consecrated ground, a field that was large and wide, with tall grass, and an oak tree thick and long. They stomped the grass flat, fixed themselves into a circle, and uttered an incantation which would contain the Supreme Being to the field. As a protective measure, they lined the trees with cornhusk masks to ensure the spirit was tethered to that plot of land. If a single chain in the row of masks was broken, there would be no guarantee, that the incantation would be enough to bind the Supreme Being. Should the ring be broken, the world could suffer an unspeakable evil it had never known.

LIFE IS BUT A DREAM

Oh, Lou- I'd like to let you know that I do not feel welcome.

All the birds, the trees, the falling snow

No they were not made for me.

> - "That Western Skyline" by Dawes

The early morning dew dripped from the sprawling spring grass in Gus Maxon's backyard. A fog blanketed the lawn and stretched out to the lake swallowing up his boathouse. His automatic coffee maker was programmed to start at five o'clock every morning and so it began percolation. The Columbian grounds casted it's roasted fragrance and permeated through thick walls and filled every room. It wafted into Gus's room, it tickled his nose and pulled him into consciousness. He sat upright and stretched his arms up for an almighty stretch. Once he was satisfied, he patted the bed with his right hand where his wife used to lay. "Linda," her name drifted from his lips as he longed for yesterday. Except for yesterday meant last year when Linda became suddenly ill and withered away in the blink of two days. Not a day would pass that Gus would not miss her. They spent 43 years of blissful marriage together, and only months into his retirement would Linda succumb to greener pastures.

He slipped out of the sheets and into the outfit of the day; long-sleeved flannel and dungaree jeans. The windows were open, a gentle gust of air drifted through the house. He slipped on a pair of wool socks and headed for the kitchen. His favorite mug labelled in bold comic sans "FISH AWAY YOUR WORRIES" was stationed next to the coffee maker. He groped the mug and the coffee pot and poured the morning stimulant. Replacing the pot, he combed his calloused work hands through his thick salty hair. He drank from his mug and let out a sharp breath through his nose. The fog was thicker than cream and the sky was smoky gray. "Nice day for fishing I guess," he whispered to himself.

Gus gulped the remainder of his morning brew and sauntered down to the basement walkout patio door. He plunged his feet into his rubber boots which waited for him beside the sliding door. He slipped on a forest green raincoat as the skies told a story of possible rain soon. A soft, cool breeze greeted him as he slid the door open – he could taste the moisture in the air. Dew drops sprinkled the tips of his boots as he kicked grass on his way down.

For thirty years, the Maxon boathouse stood tall and true. Sure, the red paint had given way to rot and worn to raw wood – the cropped-in windows chewed by weather - and the roof perforated by hailstorms, but the bones of the boathouse were healthy and would stand by itself should the rest deteriorate under the demands of Mother Nature.

The service door opened with a tug and an achy creak. Inside, the musk of thirty years twisted above the wakes below. The boat swayed with the swimming waters below, knocking against the dock like an inquisitive rap on a door. Gus loaded up the 'Sea Nymph' - as the aluminum boat had been so eloquently branded - with two fishing poles, a hard-shell tackle box with three trays, and a foam bucket containing minnows from the day before. Half of them died overnight, but he still had about a baker's dozen left. He had a 3.5 horse power 2-stroke outboard motor on the back of the Sea Nymph, but since he lost Linda to a sudden and inexplicable illness, he valued his mobility and mortality, so he resorted to using his oars to pump the heart up and to keep him loose and limber. Gus slid the two barn-style doors to their sides, the ungreased track and the weight of the doors squealed while metal grinded on metal.

The heavy fog made for a bleak landscape. No matter where Gus looked it was all bundled up blankets of either heather gray or hail white. None of this bothered Gus as he had rowed this lake back and forth, side to side, and corner to corner for the past thirty years.

Gus swished his oars through the placid waters and made his way toward Bass Bay, a nice little pocket of the lake where the reeds are dense, and the bass are plenty. Paddling along, he softly sung 'Row, row, row your boat gently down the stream," he discontinued the song in hopes to hear Linda's voice complete the second iteration, but nothing came. This was their favorite song to sing together whenever they went out to fish. When Gus was still working, they would take the boat out on Saturdays and pop on a lure and drop a line. Even in the frigid winter months they would drag their icehouse on the frozen lake and take up residence on the same patch of ice every year. They would bump along on the four-wheeler and sarcastically sing the song and giggle all the way.

Retirement had been hard for Gus. With Linda gone, there was no one to join him in small excursions, enjoy a cup of coffee, or to simply do the thing they enjoyed most, fish. He thought of buying a dog, a small one he could bring along wherever he went, or just to nestle on his lap, but he decided against it as he still enjoyed being able to do anything he wanted at the drop of a hat and the responsibility of anything outside of himself frightened him.

After ten minutes of rowing and wading through fog, Gus drifted into his cozy pocket of the lake and plunked the anchor down into the cool waters. The rope that tethered the anchor to the boat remained slack while the boat slowed to a stop. Gus grabbed the first of two rods and placed a small lead sinker on the line as well as an expiring minnow on the hook. The tiny fish was floating sideways, but still pumped his fins trying to make his way around the bucket. No amount of squirming and wiggling was going to prevent the end of his story.

He casted his line and reeled in nice and easy. As he did so, he glanced down at the second rod and thought about the times where he would prepare the line for Linda. Regardless of the countless ventures out fishing, she'd always, without fail, cringe when Gus would stick the hook through the minnow. Her boundless compassion for defenseless animals was merely one of the many reasons why he adored her so much. Many things come and go in 43 years, but his adoration for this always brought his heart peace. A memory floated into his mind and there she was teasing to him, 'I can hear him crying,' a smile plastered on her face. Gus smirked and sighed, "Linda".

His first cast out returned without any luck. So did the second, third, fourth, and fifth casts. Gus was a patient man, but today was rubbing him in a weird way. Whether it was the weather, or the delayed impact of caffeine, he was caught in the throes of indifference. Fishing no longer sounded fun. He plucked the half-dead minnow from the hook, tossed him in the water, gently rested the rod on the boat floor, and plumped down on the aluminum bench. His shoulders hung down and his back hunched forward. His throat clenched and his chest heavy, he felt warm tears squeezing their way to the corners of his eyes. He realized the reason for the apathy. It was a day, just like this, where Linda slipped into the boat, on her own while Gus tidied up the garage, and rowed into a foggy morning. That would be the last time he seen her at her healthiest before the illness ravaged her and washed away the crystal blue eyes that would gaze upon him every day. He shuddered when the memory of her coughing up blood into his handkerchief slid into his mind. "Maybe a dog isn't a bad idea," he whispered to himself.

Gus stood up. He stretched his back with his arms stretched out. He swayed his arms left and right and crossed them. Straining his muscles released the endorphins which shot out relief to every finger and toe tip. He sat back down and grunted. Instead of calling it quits and rowing back home, he picked up his fishing rod, stuck the hook through a lively minnow, and sent the line out to the deepest pocket of the lake.

After several attempts, with nothing but snagged reeds and empty hooks, Gus grew apathetic again. "Linda," he sighed, "I wish you were here." A gentle breeze swept over him, and he felt that it was a divine wind sent from Linda in an effort of easing his troubled mind. The thought comforted him.

At this point, Gus was simply soaking up moisture in the morning air. Fishing became a chore, and one he didn't intend to entertain much longer. He drew up the anchor and placed it in the back of the boat. In one swift motion he picked up the oars and dug the tip into the mucky lake floor to spin the boat around.

Swish – Swish – Swish, the oars swam through the dark blue waters. "Row, row, row your boat gently down the stream – Me-," he started the second line of the song, but was interrupted by a whistling in the distance.

"*Whoot – whoot – whoot – whoot – whoot – whoot – whoo*," the whistle mimicking the next iteration.

It continued, but Gus sang along lowly, "Life is but a dream." He figured it was either George or Todd, his neighbors whom, likewise, were retired widowers. Quickly after the closing rendition of the song he called out, "Hey there stranger!" Nothing but fog and wind responded. "George? Todd? Which one of you clowns is it?" Again nothing. Gus scratched his neck and shrugged. He figured maybe they were just out of earshot and would call again in a moment.

After a few strokes, he lost focus. The mysterious whistler disoriented Gus, and the fog thickened clouding his vision further. His head teemed with cardinal and intermediate directions weaving with one another. He was trying to remember which way to steer next, the problem was he wasn't sure which way he was facing. The sun played hide-and-seek and the clouds kept their shiny secret concealed behind their concrete walls. It was so dark that Gus lost track of time.

"Where the hell am I?" he asked himself. The silence was suffocating so the only way to know for certain he was still breathing would be to test his voice. There were nights he laid up at night in his recliner watching late night programming and not move for hours. The rise and fall of his chest had become so slow and steady it seemed to not have moved at all. "Can you gents hear me yet?" Gus tried for the widowers again. The grit in his voice thickened. He could feel the phlegm piling up in his lungs. No mistaking it today. Gus was alive, but not entirely well. He felt a cold coming on.

A crack in the concrete wall revealed the shiny secret. Thin lines of golden rays poured through them. "Ahhh, there ya are," Gus's eyes smiled brightly. Given that he couldn't have been lost long, and the sun hung halfway up the sky, it must have been somewhere around ten-in-the-morning. "East," escaped his lips and he lined his hand straight up and down as if he was cutting through the fog. "Just where I need to go." Gus groped for the oars and spun them through the waters.

His throat dried up and his muscles grew sore from rowing. He tucked the oars under the bench and stood up to do a series of arm and lower back stretches. He rotated his neck a couple times and sat down. Gus didn't want to admit it, but he was done for the day and it wasn't even noon. He grabbed the arm of the outboard motor, pulled the choke, and cranked on the starter – *lubba-lubba-lubba* – the engine teased, but he was close. A few hard tugs more and the engine coughed and rumbled to a start. Carcinogenic clouds of smoke tumbled to his face. It entered his lungs and sent him into violent hacking breaths. After a few sweeping hand-waves, pushing off the remaining puffs, he lowered the motor and set course for home.

The sun swayed between the ever-ambling clouds, the dark and light sharing shifts with one another – sometimes the light not reappearing for several minutes. Was he still heading east? The sun hid behind the formless gray slabs while his mind was breaking softly. The unease a gushing stream of hungry waters eating away at the fissures of the borders of his recollection.

Another minute passed and the sun peek-a-booed from the darkened skies – cluing to Gus that he had remained true to his direction. His steady hand had not steered him wrong, and that the steel in his bones would be resolve enough to make sure that he would make it home on this dark and gloomy day.

In this alighted shift, he saw a black silhouette of a man in a boat. The ambiguous figure floated in the amoeba-like smog, rendering it unrecognizable. He killed the motor and raised the black steel out of the water. Anxious to speak to a live person, he called out, "Hello there!" He stood there gaping at the silhouette waiting for a response. "Is that you George? Or is it Todd? You old bastards are hard to pin down when Mother Nature's a little fussy like this." The boat drifted, still advancing from the last propulsion of the motor. "Well Jesus Christ, gentleman. Can't you hear me? I'd tap dance for ya if it made a lick of a difference." Gus knew he wasn't a spring chicken and that his eyesight had been a faint cry from a silent movie these days, but he sure as hell knew that a couple of older guys, especially at the spitting distance he was to the silhouette, would need to be deafer than a pair of stones to be able to ignore his pleasantries.

He grew closer to the black outline, the center filling some, but gapped like skipped spaces of a crayon. Gus cranked his neck lower to get a better view and scrunched his face together like somehow the wrinkles in between his eyes, nose, and mouth were set to sharpen his vision. Of course, it did not, and he found himself gasping the names of George and Todd again, but half-heartedly. As if it were penciled in, sequence by sequence, white eyes and a jagged smile etched itself into the black, formless thing. The suspicion of something gone wrong crept into Gus's heart. He grabbed at the beating thing over the top of his coat, digging in with his fingertips – the knuckles rolling around, just to be sure that the hunk of meat was doing its job. It was and pounding to the tune of terror.

Soon enough the nose of the Sea Nymph drifted into the heart of the silhouette, the thin white mouth sprang into jagged lines, almost crying, but always piercing Gus's nerves giving his heart a tremble he hadn't felt until at least a year ago when Linda expired in his arms.

An explosion of wind swept over the waters. The fog burst into a million wisps and sent Gus toppling backwards into the floor of the boat knocking his head upon the bench. The boat rocked fiercely with both sides dipping into the frigid waters soaking his pants and rain jacket. The oars clanged against the aluminum walls of the boat stabbing his eardrums. The fishing poles rattled around, reel bumping against reel, poles sliding around like rams hooking horns. Kissing the floor, he could feel his breath bounce. First deep – then shallow. He could hear the tackle box spilling out jigs and lures and bobbers and lead weights. Minnows were splashing on the floor, beating their tiny fins endlessly against the boat floor trying to slip into a pool deep enough to swim and breathe.

Gus opened his eyes. His vision doubled. He blinked in fluttering fury trying to clear up what he was seeing. To his luck, he was able to settle his vision into a singular focus, but milky waves of clouds still disturbed his sight as he pushed himself up off the floor. His head rung, singing a song of pulsing concussions. Water streamed from his cheeks down to the collar of his flannel under his raincoat. His sleeves were damp, pant legs doused in shivery patches. His nerves writhed under his pink skin. When Gus eventually came to, he observed the lake and the air.

"Jesus Christ – That's gonna drum in my neck for a while," he muttered to himself gyrating an arm forward while the other nursed the swinging arm's shoulder. The fog and clouds dissipated. The skies cleared. The sun shone uninterrupted, and the sky held an astonishing Carolina blue hue. He reared his head and glanced directly into the sun. Blasts of rays seared his vision leaving him temporarily blinded. He groaned. Deep in his chest a festering clawing crawled up through the cavity and wrung his throat. Water welled in his eyes – he coughed and spit into the pit of his elbow. "Good Lord!" he was exasperated, and his hands were trembling like the last leaf in fall. Through it all, he was able to muster enough strength to drop the motor back into the water and tugged the starter. Thankfully, Gus's solitary pull was enough mettle for the motor to cough and start again.

Pipes of gold poured from the sun while the Earth cleared the leftover lake clouds. His boathouse was in plain view. The air was thin and refreshing, providing a healthy dose of oxygen for his troubled lungs.

Gus killed the motor, drew it up, and maneuvered into the boat house. He stretched out an arm and grabbed one of the poles along the boarded walkway. Using the poles of the dock, he leveraged himself out. The same festering in his chest arose, so he prepared for another coughing fit. He drew out his handkerchief and hacked into the white cloth. Once the coughing subsided, and the boiling phlegm slipped back down his throat again, he peaked into the cloth and saw bubbling red pooled in the center with speckled vermillion dots like an areola cresting a virgin's pale summer skin.

THE BONE CLOWN

So much on my mind I just can't recline

Blasting holes in the night til she bled sunshine

Breathe in, inhale vapors from bright stars that shine

Breathe out, weed smoke retrace the skyline

Heard the bass ride out like an ancient mating call

I can't take it y'all, I can feel the city breathing

Chest heaving, against the flesh of the evening

Sigh before we die like the last train leaving

    - "Respiration" by Black Star

I'm not sure what happened to Rick. He stopped showing up to work and disconnected his phone. It was two weeks of no calls, no shows and ultimately, he was let go, but my gut suggests he neither knew nor cared. He wasn't a friend, per-se, but he was a peer and someone I would occasionally talk to during smoke breaks and the intermittent breathers one would take during a task. Rick was aloof. A recluse might be a better word. No matter what the topic of conversation was, he would usually just mutter some string of pleasantries mixed in with a few curse words. I found it cumbersome to strike up conversation, but I just chalked it up to him being an oddball. All the same, he was a real, tangible person who many disregarded without a shred of consideration.

I stopped by his house, after checking the work directory for his address, just to check in with him and see if he was doing well. It was nighttime, and all the lights in the house were off. After several hard-fisted pounds on the door, it cracked open. I pushed the door further and crossed the threshold. I'd be lying if I didn't say I was impressed with his estate. The home was built circa 1900s with a lot of the original wooden floors and ornate millwork around the doors and window frames. Deep plum, billowy curtains were his choice of window treatment. The banisters leading up the stairway were thick, and the wooden spindles leading upstairs were hand-carved with voluptuous curves. His vaulted ceilings pushed up to the second floor. The house was immaculate, save for the kitchen which the fridge had been left open and spoiling milk emanated the room. I shut the pocket door, so I could close off the stench.

Instead of investigating further, I turned back towards the front of the home. A large, breath-taking bay window being the main attraction. From it, you had a terrific view of the neighborhood. This must have been his favorite place to start the day. You could sip your morning brew and behold the plentiful pines that streaked behind the houses. In front of the gorgeous window was a broad quarter-sawn oak desk with a letter set out for the world to see. Nothing else cluttered the desk. There was a sudden chill that worked up my spine and tickled the tiny hairs on the back of my neck. I got the eerie feeling Rick hadn't been here for days, probably weeks. At the very least since he had last been seen at work. Although the house was tremendous in every measure, it was still cold and hollow definitively missing the human element. Blood didn't flow through the bones of this home. It had become pale and asphyxiated.

I stared the letter down, my skin crawling all the while. The letter's icy breath called to me, summoning me to read its contents. Saying that I gave it an effort to not do so, would be a bald-faced lie. With the eagerness of a stymied toddler, my curiosity gave way and I snatched up the note from the desk. The letter read:

To whom it may concern,

It has been five years since I walked alongside the sun. In my glory days, I was a defense attorney at a successful law firm. The courtroom was my home away from home. If I wasn't there, I was here, at home, soaking up as much knowledge I could about the law. Daily, I saturated the floors in prosecutor sweat. Left and right, they would beg and plead me to stop accepting cases, but the money was so damn good, and the job was so damn easy, I couldn't help but say, "fuck you." My hubris was unbridled and carefree. I'm saying this now, as a shell of my former self with no reason to lie, and nothing to prove.

That lifestyle is now gone. None of that shit matters. I write this to merely illustrate my descent into the stirred, soulless man I am now. After the incident, everything changed. Rapidly, my senses deteriorated. I couldn't eat. I couldn't sleep. Difficult cases were hard to navigate.

My notes were cluttered, and my presence in the courtroom dissipated. Then, I was broken down to accepting smaller cases. Even then, my wherewithal to refute a claim as small as petty theft became hard to navigate, which left them walking away convicted of a crime they may or may not have committed. I took fewer cases. Lost those. My status as a top dog litigator was whittled down from a forest to a toothpick. I refused to go out for beers after the day was done. The girl I was bumping dumped me, with many choice words, and quickly took up with another lawyer at the firm. I was humiliated by my peers. Chided by the firm. Eventually, they sent me packing with backhanded "well wishes", and "get some *fucking* help loser" farewell cards.

I sought work that would occupy me through the twilight of the day through the rising sun. Eventually, I began working at a warehouse from six-at-night to six-in-the-morning. On my days off, I sleep through the day to stay awake in every inch of darkness.

All because of an itty-bitty moment, that marked me forever. I had to adjust my entire life. People might find me crazy. Think I'm out of touch with reality. They may say my story is a work of fiction and that I'm full of shit, and believe me I would if I were you, the one reading this letter. I'm prepared for the fallout. Besides, why would I care what you think? I'll be dead by the time anyone finds this.

No longer can I let it fester. All of my falling down, the contusions, the sores, the cuts, the marks, the sleepless days, the panging hunger, the dry eyes, the ringing ears, the wishing-that-shit-would-just-be-right-again, all of this shit, comes down to one Goddamn thing. The Bone Clown. Laugh, snicker, and cast shade on my name if you will. I don't blame you. It sounds absurd. It is absurd, but true all the same.

Clear as day I remember, just as if it was yesterday, I ventured out to Lake Phalen late one evening to run the track. I had just won one of my biggest cases. Through compromised evidence and a bit of sly, I got a guy off murder charges. Anyway, I was rearing the north-east bend of the five-mile track heading south was when I saw it. Two tufts of brick red hair jutting out of a massive skull streaked in my vision. Afraid to even strike a double glance, my legs stretched out further and picked up the pace. The freaks come out at night, so they say, so some freak out at the park at night in a mask was par for the course. While I was applying pressure to my eardrums, to ensure my headphones weren't slipping out, I felt a slice of air zip across my cheek. Startled, I looked to my immediate left, but saw nothing.

Scanning down the track, the figure appeared in my vision again. Ahead of me. The Bone Clown's stature loomed large, with a fiery red satin jumpsuit worn like a fitted mechanic's onesie in his immense frame. He wielded a wooden sledgehammer, the handle as thick as floor jacks and the massive sledge-head the size of a modest boulder. His head had to have been the size of a propane tank fit to light a grill for days. A crack ran down his skull revealing the vacancy inside. His craggy teeth were in perfect rows with no lips to cover them. Displayed for all to see. He angled towards me dragging the sledge behind him in the grass, cutting off my route. My mind raced faster than my pounding feet. Closing the gap, he lowered his head and kept a furious pace. With a quick pivot, I juked left, sending the sadistic clown into a skid where he narrowly avoided being dumped into the lake.

My feat was short-lived. I knew my car was on the other side of the lake. My shin splints pulsed as the acid in my stomach bubbled into my esophagus and doubled me over.

Out of instinct, I rolled into a backward somersault just in time to dodge the merciless swing of the Bone Clown's massive, splintered sledge. I popped up which gave me an advantage on the hideous thing. His endlessly black eyes tracked me like a homing missile. I couldn't tell if they were empty sockets, or the portals of hell. Either way, those eyes lusted for my death.

Back in my high school days, I played as running back for the football team. Channeling that inner-jock, I shuffled my feet to create misdirection. Instead of breaking left, I broke right, which crumbled the Bone Clown to the ground. Looking back, it was a proud moment, but the panic and fear I felt spared me no time to celebrate the small victory. I had to get to the other side of the lake.

My feet blurred beneath me as I raced to my car. It was in view, but so was that fucking clown. Once a-fucking-gain he was rushing up to me from an inescapable angle. He was inhumanly fast. His sledge was at the ready. My heart rattled in my ribcage. I could taste the iron dancing in my lungs. The acrid bite of pond scum still resonates in my nose.

As he gained ground his suit glared, blinding my vision. The shine grew close to the point where instinct, once again, kicked in and I juked towards the glare. It flew in front of me as the glare wandered from my scope of vision. Scanning left, I could see he had rolled to the ground with his sledge outside of his range of grasp. Briefly, I pulled my gaze away to track down my car. Once I had it in my sights, I darted my eyes back and saw he wasn't on the ground anymore. He was back on his feet, sledge in hand. He stood there. No longer running. No longer lifting his death weapon. Instead he rose a single hand and waved like he knew there would be a day we would meet again.

For a city block, my tires screamed as I ripped through Minnehaha Avenue. The entire way, I compulsively looked in each side view, and rear-view mirror hoping not to see the Bone Clown again. Ever again.

My mind was a wreck. I spent so many months wondering what the fuck was happening to me. All I wanted to do was go for a run that night and it ended up being the demise of life as I so intimately knew it.

Five years since that day passed, and the landscape of my life has been dramatically uprooted. No longer can I sleep at night. No longer can I rest easy. No longer can I explore the night life. Especially since yesterday.

Those two brick red locks of hair popped into my vision while I was driving to work. For the first time, I was running late, and had not been out of the door until night had fallen. On my way there, I passed the intersection of Larpenteur Avenue and Como Boulevard and there he was standing in the middle of the cemetery waving at me. Just waving. No charging. No crazed look. No other homicidal gestures. Just a simple, innocent wave with a face flatter than North Dakota. A calm, knowing look he would get me when I least expected it. The very same wave he shared that day I escaped his clutch. He found me. He fucking found me. That Goddamned face is etched in my mind, and it's only a matter of time he gets me. He found me.

I'm packing my shit up and leaving town. I'm leaving this note behind to tell my story in case you never hear from me again, and I'd count on that. I probably won't make it out of town. I'd stand up and fight, but fuck that. You haven't seen this fucking thing. Just so you have a glimpse I've left a picture I drew of him the night after my first encounter, so you can see what I'm talking about.

Whoever cares,

Rick Fretter

After reading this, I felt an urge to move about the house, but I resisted. No way could I spend another minute in this lifeless house. Especially after what I had just read. The story gave me the creeps. Not that I thought it was true by any stretch of the imagination, but it gave me a window into the warped mind that Rick harbored for so long. To his credit, the sketch he left behind jostled my nerves. No wonder he was an outcast. How could you lead a normal life, when all you obsess about was this Bone Clown?

I took Larpenteur Avenue home. Many thoughts coursed my mind while I worried at length for Rick and his mental health. It made me curious to investigate if he really was a lawyer in what he described as a past life. So much so, I pulled over just so I could Google "Rick Fretter – St. Paul". The results were jarring. I thought I was staring at a completely different person. He was clean cut, handsome, wearing a suit, smiling. He even had a Wikipedia page – albeit it only listed a few things such as where he was born (St. Paul), where he worked (Milton, Chadwick & Waters), and a few of the major cases he gained notoriety for. Below that brief description was a blurb on the mystery of his fall out and where he was now. The hyperlink was tempting to click, but I didn't want to spend all night on the side of the road.

This was definitely Rick, but not the one I knew. The one I seen punching a clock wore rags. His jackets were tattered, pants torn, shirts stained, and his shoes worn past the gum. He was unshaven, hair crawled in groups throughout his cheeks, chin, and neck. His broom-brush mustache masked his poor dental health, but not the strong case of halitosis. You could've set them next to each other in a lineup, and I never would have made the connection.

My face tingled with shock from the stark contrast of the Rick Fretter then, to the Rick Fretter now. Just then, I glanced up at the street sign. Como Boulevard. My eyes darted up and down the street signs on the same pole. Como – Larpenteur – Como – Larpenteur. My heart quickened. Then I peered left towards the cemetery. There was the head of Rick perfectly situated on a gravestone. Blood dribbled down the front and sides. I shuddered in horror. Where his body was? I wish I could tell you, but as soon as my stomach began to spoil, there he was. The two red locks jutting out of the skull and his massive splintered sledgehammer. He made a mad dash towards me. Luckily, I left the car running and was able to get out of there easily enough, but not without the courtesy of a complimentary smashed windshield.

Whatever that was, that fiendishly beast of a thing, I don't know, but what Rick had shared was true. Now, I write this just so more tales could be told of the Bone Clown should I meet a similar fate as Rick's. My heart throbs just to see a man, any man, discarded like him. The plan now is to relocate, but before I do so, I'll need to return home, pour a stiffer drink than the usual, and sort my affairs.

HELL'S HALF ACRE

Rank

Ragged

Skin sewn on sheets

Casing the barracks

For an ass to break and harness

Into the fold

  - "Queen" by Perfume Genius

T hank you for coming to my fire and sharing your stories with me tonight. It is a great pleasure to sit amongst friends and tell tales of bird-like creatures who own the sky – shredding English settlers into thin spaghetti; smoky lake ghosts concealed in sloping fogs who make you writhe and die; and creepy clowns made of bone and malice – lopping off heads and taking windshields in the name of hell-sapiens. Sure, they're fanciful stories, but they hold a special place in my cold, midnight heart. Thank you.

I guess it's my turn now. Excuse me if I get a little long-winded with this one, but it's quite personal and hits home hard and rumbles unbridled through my heart like an unchained wrecking ball. It happened to me and a friend, and to this day it remains a story I haven't shared with anyone except for those who were directly involved and to those whom it mattered most.

Many myths are molded through murmurs and misinformation out here in the clay of "God's country" but steer clear of the Big Man's kiln up above. These legends run rampant – stemming from times with highways made of dirt roads, and farmers thriving off crops and livestock. This instance is no different. Out here we talk about the bears in the woods, coyotes by the creeks, and wolves roaming in droves, but there is one that does not involve animals. One so firmly ingrained in the community, that it, in fact, turned into a warning for children to not trespass on anyone's property as it may lead to a gross misdemeanor, bear traps, or even worse – a severe departure from earth. We would take heed to keeping off everyone's land, but no lawn was more dreadful than Hell's Half Acre.

Gnarly, right? You might ask how the name came to be, but the answer bears difficulty in explanation. Like all legends, stories become subject to change over time. You've heard the stories of Vampires and Ghouls and Werewolves, but any story shared is never based solely on facts and is often up for interpretation. Each person sitting in and listening will no doubt give their orator a curious ear, but what they will hear is a tale laced with little truth and much personal fabrication to give the audience what they wish – a fantastical story of course. What I will tell you tonight are the bare facts - every raw, painful detail – and then my own account of what occurred out there on that fateful night.

A small town, much like this one, is where you'll find Hell's Half Acre. Tucked away from streetlights and bustling traffic, far past the flowing corn fields, and so deep into the country that GPS abandons halfway into the tunnels of trees and gravely roads. That is where you'll find the deserted house with a lot stretching out to a near acre.

The property belonged to Mr. Gunnersen, a tall older Swedish man with lank gray hair and arms the girth of pine trees. He was a frugal man with paranoid delusions. He believed the town's banks were corrupt and stuffing their pockets with *his* money. So, instead of storing his money with the banks, he sealed his life savings in tin coffee canisters and buried them into graves in his yard.

One day he left. Poof! Gone. The story told was that he hopped into his rusted truck and headed east out of town. Townspeople whispered about as to why he left; boring stuff like tax evasion; insurance fraud. Some even clamored that he robbed the town liquor store, however that claim was debunked after the owner vehemently denied the accusations. But the head of one rumor stood out highest of them all. He killed those who trespassed his lawn, in search of the money he concealed in his lawn and disposed of them into the culverts that ran through the wood line about a quarter mile behind his home.

One night, fifteen years ago. After school on a Friday, I had a friend come over to spend the night. Our agenda consisted of slamming pop, talking about cute girls, and diving into a hefty list of brand-new video games. Typical teenage splendor. My friend was from the cities, so he found excitement in our small town's precautionary tales. He took a special interest in this story, mainly the money buried in the ground. I made my attempts to quell his imagination, but it was useless. He found the concept overwhelmingly irresistible.

Once my parents fell asleep, we wrapped up our final round of games and polished off the remainder of our two-liter. We snuck out of my window and slid off the roof, our feet scratching louder than anticipated, for a short fall. I hoped my parents would have heard our antics in progress to stop us from this idiotic venture, but no. They were sound asleep and none-the-wiser. We set off for Hell's Half Acre. Him with giddy, fluttering feet – me with lead in my shoes.

We stayed on dirt roads and kicked rocks along the way. The moon glow held our hands along the way. Several miles passed us by, and we had arrived at last on the corner of that horrifying place. The lot was exposed to both roads with a tree line stretching the back end of the property. The damned place looked too small to really be worth the worry, but the heavy presence of dread hung in the air, congesting my senses. The air was thick, breaths coming in gulps. Weeds crawled the lawn as the grass stood tall and reached for the sky. In its formative years the house was bright white, or so the story goes, but with the natural decay of the wood siding, and the wear of severe seasons, it had washed into a pallid gray with what looked like gnawed-on slats of wood.

I thought to myself how stupid this was. I nudged my friend and said quietly, "Alright, we've seen enough. Let's go!"

He shook his head and said, "No man. You gotta be stupid to not know what I came for. I bet there's enough money out there to put me through college. Pffft, hah! You and I both know I ain't going to school after school. That's just madness."

"Yeah, you're a real Neil deGrasse Tyson," I told him. "But no, there is no way I'm going into that field. Did you not hear the stories I told you? The guy used to kill people in his yard. You might need some tutelage with that rat-brained level of comprehension. Might do you some good."

"But that's what they say... Actually, that's what *you* say that *they* say. You have no proof, and he couldn't possibly be here now anyway. How could he kill us if he's still alive? The guy would have to at least be triple digits. I don't need school to tell me the math on that. You gonna let a 100-plus year-old man take you out? Not me, man. Not a chance."

It was hard to argue with him there. Several decades ago our tri-city newspaper came out that Mr. Gunnersen had died from consumption. He had a point, but I wasn't going to concede without a hard-fought battle. Besides, I had a point of my own. "I don't know man. How do you even figure on digging up the cans, moron? With your hands?"

"No, *moron*. Look, there." He pointed to the broad side of the rotting house. Like a diamond twinkling in the sky, a spade rested against the side of the decrepit house.

"What the..." my eyes dimmed; I was dumbfounded. Still, I disregarded the notion. "Nope. Still stupid. Still not doing it. Still think you're a moron."

"Don't be such a wuss dude..." and he went off rambling about just how much of a wuss I was. He was my closest friend and he knew how to push every button and pull every lever to get my nerves into overdrive. Just as kids do, we had a spat over what we were going to do and ultimately, I caved. We made an agreement; he was going to dig – I was going to keep a lookout.

My friend led the way, hungrily staring at the open field of what could have been a mass grave of financial security. Instead of cutting across the land, we winded along the street and walked up the sidewalk all the way up to the front door. Each step on the concrete stairway leading up to the screened in porch was severed in several places. All the screens were punched out and barely hung on while the door was a gnarled thing splintering at every seam. The place gave me the creeps. I can just remember the chill of the night nipping at my nape. Every hair on my body stood at attention. My friend glanced back and made smiling eyes implying he was ready to bust down the already busted door. I furrowed my brows in disapproval and hissed, "No!" He rolled his eyes and continued to the path leading along the side of the house.

The beaming blue light from the moon highlighted the shovel that beckoned us. Every nerve was alive with fear, crawling in my skin and pleading to me to stop. I wanted to scream at him and tell him to forget the whole damn thing, but the words gripped my tongue. He strolled up to the shovel and seemed to grab it without any bit of hesitation.

Either the carbonation of the soda or the gnawing fear of my vaulted superstition spoiled my stomach as I watched him relentlessly chop into Hell's Half Acre with the spade. The grass was so tall that I couldn't tell if he was having any success. I kept my arms folded to fend off the autumn breeze and my unnerved belly, yet a tingle found a way to wriggle the notion of dread through me. Impulsively I pulled my stare up towards the tree line at the border of the premises. I peered intently, but nothing other than pine trees bare of branches and the black empty space between them filled my vision.

Again and again, he surged the shovel into the ground, but seemed to be making headway now. Dirt flew up with each upswing of the shovel. He continued at a frenetic pace. My nerves were set on edge. I looked towards the front of the house. Nothing there. Then, I swung my gaze towards the streets. Still nothing. Finally, I looked back at the tree line. My blood ran cold and my heart sank. In between two trees stood a tall man with lank gray hair and arms the size of pine trees. Mr. Gunnersen. My tongue burned as I shouted, "We gotta get the hell out of here!"

He looked back at me and said, "What? Why?"

"Look!" I pointed over to the tree line, but he was gone. My skin fell pale and prickled while I gazed at an empty space where Mr. Gunnersen had just stood. The roof of my mouth thrummed with shock, the tingles stretching from the front to the back – my gums and teeth numb to the touch.

Momentarily, he glanced to the blanched wood line, the robust moon beaming against them, but returned to his dogged efforts after the nothing but trees and gelatinous black spaces between them stared back emptily. "Look at what? Ain't nothing over there to look at. Now, do ya mind? I'm diggin' for treasure over here."

"I swear on my life, man – Mr. Gunnersen was standing right there. Right hand to God! That ugly S.O.B. stood between them two trees," my fingers gathered as a single unit – shot out as a knife guiding his eyes to where I was pointing shifting from left to right and then right to left. "You have to ditch this fantasy of finding money in the ground. He's out here lurking around, and he will kill you." The very words 'kill' chilled me and the blood drained from my face. "We gotta get the hell outta here."

"Wow, dude. I'd give you a round of applause, ya know for the overwhelming performance and all, but I'm a bit occupied here tryna get rich. Why don't you just close your eyes for a bit and give your brain a break? Startin' to see stuff and that ain't healthy.'" He kept burying his shovel and pretended my bones weren't rattling in my skin.

I screwed my eyes even tighter on the wooded area and from time to time could see a dark silhouette waving amongst the tree, but it was never as clear as it had been when I did see Mr. Gunnersen. My mind filled with monsters pouring out of the woodwork from all my favorite author's. Blackwood's indestructible *Willow* beasts emerged from long winding hidey-holes and tickled the edge of my perception while Lovecraft's shadows lurched amongst the blackness threatening to steal the very breath frothing from my beating lungs. My stomach squelched as if I were hungry, but my appetite was none.

No more heed or caution would deter him from his goal. He hacked furiously into the ground, flinging bits of earth every which way. As much as I could implore, I went on describing what I was seeing out there in the darkness of the forest, but he shrugged and ignored my pleading heart.

Clink. He hit a can. "Awwwww yeaaahhh!" He leapt for joy, whooping and hollering. Back to the ground he went tenaciously. *Clink – Clink – Clink.* The sound of the can and its contents banging around still spoils dinner for me. Even if it comes from something that isn't a can. Just the noise triggers me and brings be back to that night.

He went down to his knees and clawed feverishly at the ground – unpacking clumps of dirt handfuls at a time as if he were a burrowing mole tossing earth to the side to get down deeper. I looked back to the tree line – nothing there. The wind picked up and swirled tree branches and dead leaves on the ground. I swore there were crunchy footfalls encircling us. The wind howled a note of 'beware' in the air. My stomach folded again, anticipating the very worst. Nothing good could come out of this.

He jumped to his feet with the rusted coffee canister in his hand, hoisting it up proudly. "Hahaha," he laughed triumphantly, "I'm rich dude!" His hand slammed over the top and peeled back the lid with white-knuckled grip. Larger and larger his eyes became – seeking as if he was uncovering a chocolate bar on the verge of discovering a golden ticket. He pored inside – fingers swishing around groping wildly. Metallic *tinks* clapped up on the sides of the can while the sound of churning sand brewed in the middle. His eyebrows screwed up in confusion, slack jawed and gulping air. He raked over and over inside the can – clearly displeased with what he had found.

"What the hell, man?" he shouted with a choking cry. His wrist turned down and out came tiny pebbles and coins and hand-written receipts of bank statements – withdrawals and deposits alike – floating in the passing winds. "Didn't trust the banks? Then why the hell does he have all these crumpled up slips *and...* dirt *and...* coins. It's all trash

Even if I had cared about his sore disappointment in his findings, I couldn't have said a word. My mouth was stitched. The only thing I wanted was to be out of there, and I never wanted to catch even a faint vision of that brutish figure again.

But my wish was short-lived. Mr. Gunnersen emerged out of the black fold of night and seized him with his large hand and long, curling fingers. A single-barrel shotgun with a walnut stock and pump was firmly placed in his other. He looked at my friend with a contorted grimace. His lips parted, and breath repulsive. The teeth revealed rotted picket fences. He looked back at me and began to draw his shotgun on me, the ill-intentioned blued receiver falling into vicinity. I back peddled into a reverse run, but my feet were weak and clumsy. I tumbled backwards crashing into the ground – bouncing in each direction as if I were a puck down a Plinko board.

My thundering heart rattled in my chest and threatened to break through while I pushed dirt with my breath. With gritty earth spilling from my lips and teeth, I wheeled around, my legs twisting wildly, until I could get out of shotgun blast range. I started beating my feet against the field, each step heavier than the next, until I made it to the road and sped to the direction of a porchlight, a beacon of hope calling me down the dirt-packed street.

In my sprint there, I heard it. A shotgun blast in the distance. Though the crash of the gun was fields away – it jolted my eardrums. All over again, every internal organ writhed and spoiled inside of me. I could feel the muscles failing in my legs – tearing as I hurdled the fence and made it to the neighbor's house my body flailing at the door.

We called the police and they arrived 30 minutes later. They combed Hell's Half Acre but found no sign of a struggle. No sign of blood, or of my friend anywhere. His parents continue to search for him, but I never believed for a minute he was still out there. No shred of hope could stifle my steeping depression. He was dead, and that was probably that.

Wow. I never thought I'd have the gumption to share that story with anyone, let alone a group of strangers. I appreciate your interest and lending me your time. You ask me why I invited you over to tell you this story while we sit here at this blazing campfire – the embers popping like popcorn. I'll explain. Naturally, losing my best friend traumatized me. For years I struggled with how to handle the emotional fallout of loss and grief. As hard as I could try, I would suppress my feelings – can it in a mason jar and let it sit with Twinkies and cockroaches once the nuclear clouds settle, and that would work for a spell, but the pain was restless and when I wasn't looking it festered and stretched out their obnoxious limbs and rumbled their way through my bones. The clear answer was that I needed to make amends with the loss of my friend.

To become at peace with myself before a more aggressive, relentless depression got the better of me.

So, I bought a house out here and spruced it up. It was a hell of a lot of work, but I think it came together nicely. I replaced the chewed-up slats of siding and crumbled the front steps and poured new concrete. The porch was in fair condition, I just needed to rescreen the window frames and replace the ratty screen door. And lastly, I groomed the sprawling, untamed lawn. Below us are some tin cans and in my shed, shovels aplenty. If we can find a single can maybe we can bring my friend back. Are you guys game?

BOOK TWO

OF THE MIND

IT'S BEAUTIFUL ISN'T IT

Oh, can it be?

The voices calling me

They get lost and out of time

I should've seen it glow

But everybody knows

That a broken heart is blind

- "Little Black Submarine" by The Black Keys

1

His ears were empty, soul devoured
He wanted to hear, but was labelled a coward
His family declared to remain in the dark
To resist all the noise, and refuse to embark

In a world abound with music and birds
The cries of babies and beautiful words
Which dance in avenues and echoes in the street
Crash into eardrums with strangers you meet

No, this did not matter to family and friends
Who wished the notion to simply end
"Why" they would ask. "Out!" they would cry
With sinister barbs they would poke and pry

No answer he would give, would ever appease
The glowering crowd, with looks that could freeze
They wanted him gone, cast out forever
His family agreed, and so they would sever

No counsel, no guidance, none of the sort
"That's it," he declared. "I don't need their support"
His conviction was vivid, his conscience was clear
He went off to a consultant and demanded to hear

Not a moment was wasted!

The nurses and doctors gathered their things
and promised only a marginal sting

The needle it went
to sleep he was sent

They carved a hole in his head
and for a moment...
he was dead

They collected the paddles and charged him to life
The risks that you weigh when under the knife

His hospital stay was no more than a day
Head wrapped in gauze and was on his way

With no place to call home, he decided to roam

On a path of his own and freshly disowned
He strode in the sun and enjoyed all the tones

He took a seat in the park and the world was present
At once the noise came to play and became so pleasant

The chirping of birds and crashing of tides
The crisp autumn air and motorized rides

A plastic bag crinkled as it drifted on by
It bounced off his feet and he began to cry

Deeply sighing and choking on breath
The man looked back on the damage he left

His family shut their doors, chained the locks
Cast out their seed to grow on rocks

He clenched his jaws, and pumped his fists
Strained his heart and twisted his wrists

Burning with fury the man held firm
On a solemn vow to never return

Sweet earthly sounds put peace in his mind
He resolved to solace and placed hate behind

A collared dog walked by, a plate for her name intact
Her aptly put name "Girl", on the back owner "Jack"

Rich dark brown fur, muted by leaves and dirt
Clumps of mud wrapped 'round like a skirt

The man smiled while his companion's tail wagged
The dog rested while her playful tongue dragged

'We are one in the same, strays in the street.
Cast out by society but defy the defeat.

'All the pain we endure, the slander subjected
Is worth every bit,' the man reflected

His pleasant exchange was abruptly foreclosed
The dog shot off as if it had seen a ghost

"It's beautiful isn't it", a faint voice heard
By the man on the bench deciphering words

Alarmed, he peeled his eyes from the ground
He searched for a body, but none could be found

"Yes, it is," he replied to the voice as to be polite
Still confused from this body escaping his sight

His untrained voice was muffled and muddled
akin to a child learning to speak

It boomed and bounced and balanced and bubbled
but hinged on frail and weak

The whisper in the air continued to breeze
"Does the sound of my voice put you at ease?"

"Yes" he replied with a puzzled look in his eyes
How the voice could understand him was a surprise

"Have you no lodging? No kin to connect?"
Said the soothing voice with the utmost respect

He shook his head, touched by bewilderment
The air grew warm, with the voice's sentiment

"I'll be your companion and be your best friend
I'm on your side 'til the path heads to an end

"Your troubles, your worries, and even your quest
I'll be there forever, I have just one request"

He wondered a moment, then pondered a lot
The voice was so nice, so he figured "Why not?"

"Thank you, my friend, it means a great deal"
The man deduced the voice might not be real

Perhaps it was a sign from above, he supposed
A confidant who existed without skin or neat clothes

"What is your request?" said the man without aim
"Please, take a walk with me right down the lane"

The Whisper Continued

"A man is starving at the end of this block,
would you stop at the market to feed him?
I would but have no money nor stock
It has been some time since I have seen him"

The man gave it a thought before he began
How could he help this unfortunate man

If he could barely afford to feed himself?
"I must retrieve it quietly from the shelf"

He roams in the store with only one goal
Walk away with an apple and hope no one will know

He picks it and places it in his coat sleeve
and moseys on out without a peep as he leaves

Suddenly, the brown dog appeared
In a much different mood

Her lip curled and snarled in fear
"When did she get so rude?"

"The dog is rabid, kick her away"
The voice made his claim strong
"But the dog was so nice earlier today
I'll just send her along"

The man waved her off and the scruffy dog ran
Back to the mission to feed the hungry poor man

They searched left and right from sky to ground
He panned further, but the poor man was not found

"I swear he was here"
The voice rang clear

The man grew concerned, he was lost and confused
"I suppose you should eat it" the whisper issued

The man would be remiss to let the tender fruit spoil
So, he sank in his teeth to savor the trouble and toil

A mission complete...

2

At least the hearing man thought
The whisper had an alternate plot

"A cry, do you hear it?" asked the voice quite strong
"Yes," the man lied, but decided to play along

"A woman and child have just been robbed,
and I spotted the coward who done it
Capture the wretch and dispatch his last breath
'fore another comes and does it"

He shot off like a rocket,
Thinking only of what was righteous and just
How he soon would catch him
and the might he would thrust

He maneuvered the crowds and kicked-up birds
Scrambling to snatch-up the thief
He closed the gap
Clasped his back
And cast him into a pile of leaves

He grasped his shoulder and flipped him over
And employed a rock from nearby
No bag nor carriage
Just a man disparaged
Professing his will to survive

His stomach lurched and upset his system
The accosted man began to pray
Hissing dismissal
The hearing man whistled
"Go! Leave! Be on your way!"

The accused scampered off with a hump in his back
Still baffled and puzzled by the man's attack

The whisper chirped, "What is the matter with you?
He's gone to rob another
Have you no concern for what else he may do?
The next may be your brother"

"I wish he would", the man returned
"My family is as good as burned"

A nibble of intrigue for the whisper to consume
"A bit of discourse, of course, what did they do?"

The man told the tale of his barring

Surplus of tears and the fateful scarring

Expelled and exiled

The whispers voice smiled

"A story so impossibly jarring"

The hearing man continued

"In the center of my heart is a flame which blazes with
contempt!
Why must I be the sole bearer of pain while they remain
exempt?"
What a Fine Time for the Voice to Interject

"They deserve to feel your pain
Since you had none of this coming
What better way to demonstrate
Then to watch their blood running?"

"What?" questioned the man, struck by the nerve
He yielded to see what purpose this would serve

"They have forsaken you! Your soul tormented!
Labelled you as twisted! Demented!

"Zero concern for your wellbeing!
Now you are on the street!
It is clear to me what I am seeing!
Do not let them revel in their defeat!

"Justice must be served! Send them to their grave!
Let God have mercy on how they behave!"

Rankled by the voice like a knife buried deep
Words twisting, allowing the notion to steep

Repulsed and intrigued all in the same breath
What could he achieve in his family's death?

Without breathing a word, the voice replied
"Imagine how free you would be if they died?

"Their chilling words and barbs of disdain
Your efforts will render the evidence plain

"The look on their face when your revenge is exacted
Will replenish your soul", the haunting voice enacted.

3

'Is this a twisted figment of my imagination?
Or a burning call awaiting implementation?

'The voice has placed a wager on my Family's head
Should I act with vulgar distaste?
Have I entered a point in which they are better off dead?
Could I move with exaggerated haste?'

The wind picked back up

The dog returned, a blaze of fury in her eyes
Coupled with a growl which doubled the surprise

He called the dog closer, but it gruffly declined
The dog anchored its heels with a curve in her spine

"I told you the dog is mad! It will soon lash out!
There is nothing for you to think about.

"She will strike and gnaw from skin down to bone
And develop a taste for blood, but not yours alone

"She will then commence on a rampaged tour
End this dog's life, before she attempts to end yours!"

For a moment the breeze had ceased to blow
The dog sensed a moment of calm
He went to his knees
Brushed off the fleas
And placed the dog's chin in his palm

"Good girl," The man spoke with gentle care
"I must admit you truly had me scared."

The dog whimpered and licked the man's arm
Who now felt the dog could have never done harm

The wind flared, and the voice roared back
"Finish her now before she attacks!"

In a blind, blood-surging rage, the dog bounded
A mouthful of the man's arm in her bite
Stunned by the skirmish, his heart pounded
The man twisted her neck and ended the fight

Shuddering from the crack of the bone
From this dog who suffered her untimely death
Consumed by woe, the man felt alone
On the account of the dog's extinguished breath

"There, there," the voice consoled the man
"You know this was never my plan

"I want what is best for you, I'm sure you know
That dog was tricking you and it put on a show

"Please know that I meant to do her no wrong
But we must continue, we have to get strong"

The man nodded and breathed not a word

Remembering the voice's exigent request
The man consented to the arduous quest

And so, he set forth to his former home
The voice nestled firmly inside of his dome

His march back to the family took no time at all
The tick of his watch echoed like sirens down a hall.

The Earth exhaled and swept the pines in a westerly bend
"Are you ready for glory?" whispered his intangible friend

He neared the driveway, his pulse grossly quickened
"I am" he sighed although his nerves never thickened

The pit of his gut twisted at the thought of raw murder
Pain in his chest wrenched as his mind scaled further

He gathered a branch from the edge of the lawn
Wielded like an armored knight, his sword drawn

The beat of his heart was there in his feet
Courage and nausea battled against heat

Trembling with fear, he could hardly stand
With his nose to the door, he raised his hand

BOOM... BOOM... BOOM...

He pounded the door
His brother alerted by vibrations in the floor

"Yes, yes!" urged the malevolent voice
"The time has come! You have made the right choice

"Remember! No fear! Recall what they have done!
You are vindicated! You are free! Your battle is won!"

The knob rattled and jolted the drums of his ears
The groan of the door hinge needled his fears

Every nerve twitched, and his body convulsed
He felt he couldn't do it, his conscience repulsed

The door swung open; his brother stood still
"Now!" boomed the voice with a compacted shrill

Paroxysm of anger had seized him
Death to the family that released him

All the memories surged back
His mind stumbled and cracked

He wrangled the branch with both hands and then
Thrust the branch through his brother's abdomen

The sounds of his brother gasping for air
Reaching for help that was not there

Gargling blood, Scratched floor, shifting and writhing
Agonal breaths signified his brother was dying

Abhorred by the noise, his eyes raged with tears
"My brother!" he wailed with a body of fears

A moment passed, still no word from the voice
"Why did you lead me to this detestable choice?"

He mawkishly gazed while his brother lay dead
It was apparent to him now; the voice had fled

From out of the foyer, his parents ran
Their searching eyes scanned the man

Their hands shook violently, expressing their pain
The man disappeared like water down a drain

4

His hands were stained with the blood of his brother
Flashing back to the cries of his father and mother

His heart was burrowed in the dirt of sorrow
What he had done made him plead for tomorrow

Running and running until he could not breathe
'Til the edge of the woods where he made his reprieve

"It was you!" he screamed, "Why did I listen?
You led me astray in this warped perdition!

"The poor man did not exist! The robber was bogus!
The dog had tried to warn me, but I lost focus!

"And my brother! Dear brother! Now, he is dead
How could I be fooled? So easily misled?

"Now, where are you? Have you nothing to say?
Nothing to glean from this abysmal display?

"I am a shell, a pawn, a leaf in the wind
You expended my energy, beggared within

"You'll never return and just to make certain
I'll rip out your muscle and close this curtain."

With his final threat he clawed at his face
Digging into skin where the implant was placed

Through hair and skin, he did tear and rip
Blood streamed down from his ears and lips.

He unearthed the device through tireless prying
And grew faint from all of the trying

His eyes tenderly shut with peace in his action
On the side of the road he reached satisfaction

5

The next time he opened his eyes
He was met with a pleasant surprise

The nurses and doctors swarmed his bed
"He's alive!" he had believed they said

They chittered about but nothing was heard
At last, his ears devoid of word

A lucid memory recalled the voice
He loathed his reprehensible choice

To saunter so loosely into squalid rage
A regret to bemoan in his hospital stage

For now, he would rejoice in the silence and respite
Breathe . . . Relax . . . "It's beautiful isn't it"

MEAT HOOK MAMBO

Three guns and one goes off

One's empty, one's not quick enough

One burn, one red, one grin

Search the graves while the camera spins

Chunks of you will sink down to seals

Blubber rich in mourning

They'll nosh you up, yes, they'll nosh the love away

But it's fair to say, you will still haunt me

- "Tesselate" by Alt-J

THE PRECINCT

"Look at this fucken mess..." Detective Ham Seller muttered under his breath. For the third day in a row the police officer on coffee duty made the thickest, crude oil known to man in the western hemisphere. He jabbed his spoon into the mass in his cup, half-expecting a muddy hand to reach out and swallow the head whole. "Nothing can save this damn thing," he said after cutting it with week-old half and half in the office fridge. But the coffee wasn't the real problem. He drank this 'shit coffee' all day just to keep owl-eyed while they pored over the rash of severely disturbing cases that occurred over the past couple of weeks.

First, he kicked off last Monday with a Clown suicide. Well, an act of civil justice gone wrong. Ram Jam the clown, no affiliation with the classic rock band, was soaring high at the local clown academy. He was at the top of his class and garnered national attention from the likes of the "Ringling Bros." and "Barnum and Bailey". How one manages to get on such a radar and garner such national attention, no one knows. At any rate, Ram Jam worked tirelessly in his craft, flipping hats, swinging brooms, and drumming up some quippy one-liners just so when it did come time to intern with the likes of the aforementioned big-time circuses, he would be ready to paint his face and get to work.

However, the streets had been festering with creepy clowns as of late. The remake of the Stephen King classic *It* had just hit theatres and the desperately young and dumb teenagers took to the streets with their masks and recently dropped balls, running rampant with skateboards and mock weapons never intending to stain any streets red (however, there was that one clown someone had phoned in about barking hysterically into the receiver about a severed head in a graveyard which nothing had turned up in cursory investigations).

For an up and coming clown, this became an issue for Ram Jam as he claimed they were, "interfering with people's livelihoods", told by fellow classmate Clippie, a clown-in-training who looked to Ram Jam as a mentor and a close friend.

In an effort to sway these delusional teens from dressing up as creepy clowns, Ram Jam commandeered a mannequin from his 'Perfect your Look at the Circus' classroom and took some choice wardrobe items. He stopped at a thrift store and picked up a cheap mask mimicking Sweet Tooth from the Twisted Metal game series, sunken eyes, bulbous vermillion nose, and teeth like broad piano keys. He stopped at a local home improvement store and picked up a one-hundred-foot length rope, thick enough to hang a few mannequins.

The Clown academy was nearly six stories high. Taking the elevator, he brought up all said items, fashioned a "creepy clown", tied the rope on the dummy, and put a note in the dummy's pocket saying, "I had to do it and I'm sorry I couldn't take anymore". He tossed the dummy over the edge to let it hang. Problem was, Ram Jam forgot to tie the other end of the rope. Immediately recognizing his error, he chased the mannequin as it cascaded down the side. He rode the sliding rope on his fingertips. They strummed along until the whipping rope finally conceded and burned into grip. The rope twanged a haunting note and the weight of the freefalling makeshift clowns tugged Ram Jam over the edge. Witnesses all concurred that the noise the bright, young clown made as he was suspended in air, momentarily, still chills them. His bones became dust and blood painted the sidewalk, school façade, and the already red fire hydrant. Fortunately, for the mannequin, it's fall was broken by a tree and held together quite well considering the other involved. The note intended for the dummy floated on down and conveniently landed nearby to give enough doubt that it could have been anything else other than suicide.

Later in the week, the police department received a call from a frightened neighbor. She claimed to not have seen her neighbor in two weeks. She was alarmed when a rancid smell emanated from the backyard. The neighbor she referred to was Chloe who was known amongst her neighbors as a foster for stray dogs. Her heart bled for the discarded and misplaced, and as a lover of animals, she vowed to be the person who would answer the call should everyone else let the line ring. Detective Seller got a call from the police department after they determined some foul play was involved.

He recalled it was a windy day. The doors had been left open in Chloe's home, lending the air an opportunity to create sneezing gusts of the repulsive smell throughout the home. Seller waded through the cloud of stink as he meandered through the house and out to the back patio. There she was, well, at least what was left of her. She was mostly bones with flecks of meat between a few ribs and the groin region. She was splayed on the steps coming down the short deck; half on the steps, half on the concrete. He observed two wine bottles strewn on the table at the top of the deck. He then saw the minefield of dog shit strewn across the lawn.

It didn't take long for Seller to figure it out. This was a clear-cut accident. Albeit a fantastic one, but one all the same. Chloe slipped and fell, cracked the back of her head and neck. Likely, she died instantly, and after a few days of being outside in the soft heat with nothing to eat, her nine dogs worked up an appetite. After their meal *de la Chloe*, they must have been hungry again. One, or a few, of the dogs chewed holes big enough through the tall red oak fence paneling and turned her backyard into a Baha Men concert.

Seller drew the coffee cup to his lips while he reflected on the events. Waves of the pungent coffee wafted into his nose resembling notes of the flattened clown and doggy bag leftovers. He choked down some more of the sludge. As much as his stomach protested the black stuff, it mixed in well enough with the rest of the beef jerky and like indigestible items floating around the sack of stomach acid, creating a perfect bouquet of unhealthy and spoiled foods. Enough to keep the cows from coming home.

"Hey Butcher! You ready to hop on this next one or what? Waiting on *you*." Seller's partner, Detective Cline Towers, came up with the nickname 'Butcher' on the account of Seller's unfortunate birth name, Ham Seller. Much like his name, Towers was tall, and his voice boomed deep and smooth. He was a sarcastic sort, jabbing his acrid tongue anywhere he saw fit. The two had been partners for the better part of five years now, so the insults flew back and forth freely.

"Do you mind? I'm trying to poison myself here," Seller's joked as he tipped his mug up for another swig while popping his middle finger in the air with the same hand. "Besides, what's the rush?" he asked while gulping down another lump of office coffee waste.

"'Member that dude whose been hanging mutilated bodies on meat hooks?"

"Yeah," he almost forgot about that. His mind had been preoccupied with Ram Jam, Chloe, and even a lesser case including a Mr. Tramper, a middle-aged man murdered by a teenager. For the past month there had been a depraved lunatic putting on a show for the police department. Two different bodies were sadistically dismembered at two separate times. One in a warehouse the other in a private hangar. The artwork was still the same; limbless torsos hung on a meat hook with care. "Yeah, how could I forget such an artist?" he said incredulously.

"Well, he's back at it again. This time he set up shop at that old, abandoned hardware shop down on Stinson," Towers snapped his finger trying to draw the name out of thin air. "You know the one... Weird fuck ran the place..." He snapped more fingers. "Damn man, you know the one. Caught for exposing himself to a group of old ladies at the church down on Lincoln Avenue?"

Seller's stared at him blankly. Not because he didn't know who it was, he just loved watching his partner struggle like this. In fact, he knew precisely who he was talking about. Samuel Rudd. He ran a hardware store named Nutz and Boltz. "Doesn't ring a bell," Seller said with a curling smirk just to further agitate him.

"I can tell by that silly ass grin on your face that you know *exactly* who I'm talkin' about," Towers said with wide perceiving eyes. He snapped another series of fingers. "Rudd! Hahaha, yeah... that sick bastard. What was that commercial he had goin'? That catchy tagline at the end?"

"Stop by and we'll show you our Nutz & Boltz," Seller snickered as he spoke, releasing short bursts of air through his teeth.

On the other end of the conversation, however, Towers shrieked. From the way he talked, you would not surmise a man of his stature could produce such a noise, but there he was reveling in the sheer irony of Mr. Rudd in a pitch just shy of a boiling teapot. He bellowed a sigh as his laughter petered out and said, "Never underestimate the fickle finger of fate. Well, Mr. Butcher, you done with that toxic sludge yet? I know it's your drug of choice, but we gotta beat feet and get the hell up outta here. Misery and misfortune is a motherfucker waiting on a steel hook for you."

Seller hovered his nose over the coffee, sniffed deep, and mildly retched. A sharp buzz rang in his ear which snuck into his temples. He scrunched his face in reaction to the pain.

"You okay, Butcher?"

"Yeah, yeah," he said as he plopped the cup down. Shrugging off the headache, he rose from his chair and said, "Let's kick this pig."

ABANDONED HARDWARE STORE

T hey arrived, the city block filled with crooked neck street gawkers, and absentee students catching blips of updates on their social media platforms. The 2,500 square foot compound was bordered off by wooden barricades and tall, cylindrical traffic cones. They threaded the cones and barricades with enough caution tape to wrap around the site several times over. The entry points were manned by about a dozen police officers or so. Hundreds of civilians hovered, bounced, and pressed against the boundaries as they peered into the abandoned hardware store.

Seller and Towers swam through the crowd like a couple of bass squirming through thick reeds. They flashed their badges to the officers at the entry points and shimmied past the barricades. Upon passing the police officers on duty at the door, the officers explained there wasn't any trace of 'Who done it. Just a rotting piece of meat on a hook' was the most of what was worthy of being written down in Seller's little book of notes.

There it was again, the undulant wave of rotted flesh, now joined by the teeming stench of piss and excrement. The seasoned veterans broached the entrance undeterred. Wasn't the first time they smelled this level of nasty. One of their first cases together was a murder/suicide where the wife was the assailant. Lopped off the husband's penis, shoved it down his throat, then commenced slitting his throat to pull the phallus out that way. She watched her lover die. Filled with remorse, she turned the blade on herself and plunged it deep into her left breast making her mark with precision. They were found five days later with the buzz of bile and body decay. Till death do us part, and all that.

The walls were touched by age and mold; what must have been a bleach white was now a yellow ochre, and the vinyl tile flooring peeling wax. Black tiles faded to dirty dark gray. Bisque tiles turned to a smoker's mustache yellow. The counters and the shelving were still intact, just now covered in a film of dust and lint. Over the years, with the shop being shut down and all, nothing was disturbed. Well, nothing, except the center of the store.

"Well look at this shit here," Towers boomed while gesturing to the leftovers of the poor soul. "Like déjà vu up in here!"

There was the victim dangling on the cold steel meat hook. The chain had been strung up through the open ceiling tiles and wrapped around the rafters, about 20 feet from the floor, but still carefully measured to ensure the victim would be in plain sight. The body gently swayed to and fro with the passing wind of people in motion, but never enough to cause concern, as the bottom of the torso twisted in front of Seller's face.

It was a hack job, with every pun intended, just like the rest of the senseless murders, as evidenced by the multiple chopping marks made on the shoulders and pelvic area. Below him was a small card table, no chairs, littered in poker cards, cocaine and a rolled up one-hundred-dollar bill.

"Amateur," Seller said of the killer then turned to the forensic analyst on the job and asked, "How long you figure he's been stuck up there?"

"Up *there*? Probably 36 hours, give or take a few," the forensic analyst answered. He had red medium length, messy hair. Brown eyes. Average build. Glasses. Nothing special. "But if you ask me, I would say that I think he's been dead for a day or two longer."

"What makes you think that?" Towers interjected, seizing the attention from Seller. "What about the card table and the drugs?"

The forensic analyst pivoted towards Towers, acknowledged his presence, then pivoted again towards the front of the victim and postured, "The level of decay is pretty progressive. Granted the atmosphere is conducive for bacteria to swarm the corpse, but all other signs point to approximately a week. If you look at the cuts on the body and the injury on the back from the hook, you can see the difference." He led the detectives behind the body and pointed to the penetration of the hook. "Hardly any blood on the meat hook, and *usually* whenever you have an open wound it takes *so* long for decay to ravage the injury. The one here on the back has started to rot, but not to the degree as the others. As far as the card table goes, it appears to be a distraction. There's a dead hooker in the bathroom, but likely unrelated to the event. No wounds other than bruised veins and track marks. Needle, spoon, lighter, tie-off next to her. Obvious overdose. Dead for maybe four or five days. Good thing though, huh? One less dead hooker in the world."

"Yeah, sure man," Towers said pushing the last statement aside. "We've been at the other sites but haven't had as much insight from the other analysts as you've given us. We appreciate it."

"Oh," the forensic analyst said, startled by the compliment, "you're welcome."

The gaze between the two lingered a little outside of the comfort zone so Towers spun around to the front of the body. He remarked, "Hey Butcher! You see this yet? This dude's got balls for eyes." Indeed,

THE PORTABLE HORRORS OF C. J. BOW

the killer had rearranged the genitalia to display testicles for eyeballs. They dangled forward mimicking a novelty pair of springy spectacles you get at a joke store. Except a little bloodier, and a little less funny.

Sellers walked around to the front. "That's new," he said. Nothing Seller ever said came with inflection. Everything was just what it was. No surprises, no let downs. Life was just a happy, plain medium. He aimed to keep it this way, regardless of the meat hook mambo him and Towers were conducting now.

"Any takes on the eye-*balls*, Mr. Analyst?" Towers asked as he nudged a not-so-subtle elbow.

"Thankfully, that isn't my purview," he replied. "Probably just another sick fuck with a severely demented mind. I'm kinda thinkin' the dead hooker in the bathroom might be worth a second look though." A smile jerked up at the corners of his mouth, as he let out a snicker. He gathered his kit and samples from the immediate area and stacked them neatly in the foam form insides of the hard-plastic case. "I've gotta head to the office and run some of this data. Have a good night guys."

Both detectives waved him and his strange indication to the hooker off. The prostitute meant nothing to them, and clearly seemed to be a distractor to what they were meaning to accomplish.

"Let's follow suit," Seller said. "Something tells me we can learn more back at the office than at this Picasso poser poker table ensemble. Might head back tonight just to scope it out after the circus clears and the musk settles. You game?"

"Nah man, I got a date tonight!" Towers responded with exuberance.

"No shit, huh? Who's the lucky girl?"

"The lucky girl?" Towers sneered. "I don't need a girl. Shit, I got a six pack and a couple Ambien. Time to slip into a coma and forget the world, ya dig? I need some Z's and a warm bed to ease my troubled mind."

Seller smiled. "Well *excuse* me. I guess I should have known better than to think that some broad would waste a moment to even think about spending some time with a morbid mind such as yours. Let's get back to the office then and maybe we can see what we can see, y*a dig?*" he mocked his partner.

As they made their way out of the building, Seller felt a pulsing headache surfacing – reminiscent of the buzz he encountered earlier. Increasingly getting worse and worse, he searched his pockets but could not find any ibuprofen in any of them. "Let's stop at the gas station on the way back," Seller said. "My fucken heads throbbing. Need some drugs and coffee to settle my nerves."

"Don't worry, Butcher. I got you. I got some drugs that might do you right. And I got some coffee in the car to choke it down," Towers said.

Slipping through the crowd, the two got into Towers' black sedan and faded into the shadows of the passing buildings as they headed back east towards the station

11:35 P.M.

Seller departed from the office after a grueling day putting the puzzle together of the meat hook murders. He and Towers got lost in a sea of grotesque pictures fit for the likes of serial killers and horror fiction freaks. They pinned them up. Drew string from one to the next. Mapped out the proximity of each murder. Researched the interconnectedness of the names of each victim. Hoping to land at least a sixth degree of relationship. Aside from the Christian belief that we are all children of God and are related because of Adam and Eve, there was nothing to weave the string of murders together. No matter the lens they chose to see it all through, they couldn't narrow it down any further than the simple fact that it was the same person committing these gruesome murders.

Seller had his final cup of coffee for the night and headed back out to the abandoned hardware store, while Towers nursed his exhaustion with booze and sleepy pills. The moon was concealed by the voluptuous clouds in the darkened sky. There was a precipitous drop in temperature since the detectives arrived on the scene approximately ten hours ago. It was cold enough for Seller to see his breath, button up his woolen pea coat, and reach for a beanie had had stashed in his glove compartment. He stretched it beyond his ears. With a cherry blossomed nose, Seller pulled up, in his brand-newish pickup truck, to the compound clear of crooked neck street gawkers, and absentee students.

The streets were hollow, and the reverberation of his idling car permeated the block. It was dark and dead outside of the building. There was no one to be seen. A stark contrast to what he had seen earlier in the day. Not even a streetlight could spot him on his way into the store. He killed the engine and made his way into the building with his Maglite flashing brightly along the way.

The Maglite lit the way, casting various suspicious shadows behind empty shelving, and endcaps. His footsteps clacked along. *Clack. Clack. Clack.* The stench of the mess the killer left behind was still present. The main source of the nocuous smell had largely diminished with the removal of the hooker and meat hook victim. Seller made his way to the center of the store and stood before the table where the drugs had been earlier in the day. He scaled his gaze upwards and noticed the meat hook was no longer dangling from the rafters.

Frames of the hanging body slid into his mind. Each frame crashed in, like a man shoved into a mosh pit, as the previous frames rumbled out with the tenderness of a century-old, rusted train. The imagery seized his vision. In his mind's eye an indistinguishable figure was wrapping a chain, with the meat hook on the end, around the metal rafters of the store. The figure stood on the poker table while he wrapped the chain into a knot and tugged at the chain for a weight check.

Seller became dizzy shortly afterwards and took a knee. Nausea clawed at his stomach like buzzards pecking at antelope carcasses.

Some reprieve came when the visions ceased, but the disruption inside rumbled along. Seller returned to his feet with a low-hanging gut and interrupted focus, but he was prepared.

Observing the dark, empty space with swerving eyes, he peered in with his Maglite illuminating the bathroom doors. On the left side, the unassuming Men's door. On the right was the women's facility where the dead hooker had been. He ventured over hoping to find a missing link between the hooker and the meat hook victim. The two detectives had pretty much written off the dead hooker at the scene of the crime, but he felt it required his due diligence.

Suddenly, from the right, shelving was rattling up and down on their stands. Seller drew his side arm with his Maglite fixed above it. "Whoever you are, come out nice and easy, and I won't redecorate the store an unmistakable color of red," Seller commanded.

The sound of pounding footsteps slapped on the floor as the unidentified person ran along the backside of the shelving. Sellers sidestepped into a gallop down the aisle with his sidearm trained towards the end of the row. His heart hammered as he neared the endcap. The footsteps stopped, but the shelving shook violently. Seller pulled his gaze from the end of the aisle, leaving his weapon and Maglite trained in the other direction, and looked at the top of the shelving where it was shaking. A naked man had clambered up and stood above him. He hollered as he descended with the will of the Lord and drove his shoulder into Seller's chest knocking him backwards into the adjacent shelfing creating a cascading effect of rows clinking back like dominos. The force of the attack broke his weapon and Maglite from his grasp, sending them crashing on the vinyl floor while Seller bounced off the racking and belly-flopped forward.

The Maglite revolved in rapid succession flashing the naked man's face, masking his identity. Whomever it was, Seller did not anticipate a nude dude strutting his stuff in a birthday suit in his contingency plan. Steadily, the Maglite lulled to a stop and zeroed in on the man's face.

"*Samuel Rudd*," An uncharacteristic wave of shock came over Seller as he uttered the name. "What the *fuck* are you doing here?"

"How come you didn't notice me earlier," Rudd asked with contempt in his eyes. There he stood with red medium length, messy hair. Brown eyes. Average build. Glasses. Nothing special.

Another wave encumbered Seller, "Well it was difficult since your dick wasn't hanging out then," Seller sneered as he leveraged his weight with his elbow pushing off the floor. He rung his bell somewhere amidst the commotion of ping-ponging off the racking and floor. Pain coursed his occipital lobe and throbbed at his neck. The stabbing of nerve endings crashed together "You took quite the career path I see. Where did you go to school for that? Where can I go to learn about building a business, creating a client base, whipping your dick out *for* elderly parishioners, becoming a *for*-ensic analyst, and then whipping your dick out *for* a detective? Is that an MBA thing, or..."?

"You're so *goddamn* funny," Rudd snarled fiercely. "You know, I worked really hard getting to this point. Making this perfect set up, and it all went to shit." He babbled on, grumbling about incoherent things.

"What are you talkin' about man?" Seller asked while shielding his vision from the flaccid dangly thing extending from Rudd's groin. "And God alive can you put some damn clothes on? You've made your point, it's cold outside."

"Keep insulting me," Rudd threatened, "and just see how this evening turns out for you Mr. Seller, or Butcher, or whatever the hell they call you."

Seller felt the sudden urge to clap back sarcastic remarks about who he really is, and mutter back and forth with the origin of his nickname. Instead, he said, "Alright, alright, what's your damage?"

Rudd's arms were slack, but his fists were cranked tight. Before he spoke, he gnawed at his bottom lip until it cracked and split. "That dead hooker in the bathroom was going to be my claim to fame. At least the catalyst, ya know. I was gonna be the one on the *fucking* news as the

'Hooker Tooker', expelling the filthy whores from the streets. I overfed her some H and watched her mouth foam like an unclean shore. I stood there while the luster of her green eyes went gray and her skin went cold. It gave me a sense of purpose. To purge the world of this meaningless trash that litters the street, infecting and re-infecting their clients spreading the plague of sexually transmitted diseases and straining the social fabric of our community. I'm sweeping the streets, and even though that was the first one, there were more to come. Then this jackass, whoever he is, cutting up dead bodies and putting them on hooks, had to steal the show. Who even does that anyway? And how the hell did he wind up at the exact place I killed a hooker. Kismet, I guess. Regardless, you guys couldn't peel your fucking eyes from the guy on the hook for *one* second to look at the dead bitch. All I wanted was some notoriety. The late-night news debating on the morality of my doings. A vigilante or some shit. I wanted to be controversial for fuck's sakes, but fuck it, because who cares about a dead whore when you have something more visceral like a dead body on a hook. Just my Goddamn luck."

"Well, well, well," a booming voice blasted from out of the darkness. A beam of light shot Rudd in the face. Towers had been looming from a distance catching every bit of the conversation. "What do we have here? The forensic analyst, or should I say Mr. Nutz and Boltz. In the flesh. Didn't place you as a hooker killer. Or what was it you called yourself? 'Hooker Tooker'? That's just bad man. You should go back to the drawing board with that, either that or probably just go back to flashing little, old ladies."

Rudd, startled, tried reaching around for the nearest object. Being in the buff failed to provide adequate storage for weapons. In Rudd's frantic search for something nearby, he glanced up at Towers for a sliver of a second. Towers' sidearm was already drawn. He squeezed the trigger with the meaty portion of his finger and placed a bullet squarely in Rudd's teeth, blasting enamel like shrapnel up and down his brain stem. Rudd collapsed like a sack of stones. He was dead instantly.

"What the fuck, Towers?" Seller exclaimed. "Why did you shoot the poor bastard? It's not like he was going to do anything. He was just grandstanding." An inkling draped over Seller that the grandstanding would have soon turned violent.

"You know he was about to attack me," Towers responded, "right? Besides, Butcher, you should be thanking me. He was coming after you next. Unless you like looking at shriveled up little ding dongs, then you can stay mad." He bellowed in laughter.

"You just crack yourself up, don't you?" Seller still sore from the naked man crashing into him. "Help me up, would ya?"

Just as Towers extended his hand, he rescinded the offer. "You know what, hold on a minute," Towers said.

"C'mon man, don't be a dick, just help me up."

"You got a lot of fuckin' nerve coming back out here Butcher," Towers tone changed. Gone was the jovial wave of his cadence. This was a statement of severity. One of animosity.

Seller wasn't sure where this was leading next. The pulsating pain of images shuffling through his mind returned, this time with increased intensity and merciless in its pace. Seller wanted to say something, but he couldn't muster anything but groans.

"I don't think you understand just how predictable you are, Butcher. Every time a dead body surfaces, especially lately, with these pieces of meat swinging like dicks in a Magic Mike movie, not like Nutz & Boltz guy, you always wanna come back out and take a *second* look at things."

"It's my fucken job, Towers." Seller's palpitations increased while he stretched out his arm to grab his sidearm.

"No no no no no nooooo," Towers said softly as he pulled out his pistol and locked Seller in his sights. "Let's not do this. At least not this way. You just sit tight while I hypothesize. Can you do that Butcher?"

Seller nodded. His mind was battling the constant shuffling of frames. He winced as each frame bounced in and out. He couldn't make out what was going on in these images, but it was much like his current surroundings.

"Thank you," Towers smiled as he shifted his weight and began to pace. "Now, we've been friends for a while. 'Bout five years, right?"

Again, Seller nodded. "I'd say that's fairly accurate. Is there a point you're driving at? I'm getting fairly bored."

"Yeah, that's right. In that time, we've covered a lot of homicide cases together, you and I, and for some reason I just started getting the feeling like something wasn't right. Now I know that comes with the territory. This job gets messy, the hours get long, and your mind starts doing things to you. Things that don't happen to regular folks. In doing so, things become easier to do. More justifiable in your eyes. You trackin'?"

"Not at all," Seller said as he braced his temples. The images in his mind were becoming sharper and more vivid. They accelerated to a speed of a film reel. Each slide slicing his mind like a fine razor. Surely at this point, his brain was hemorrhaging. Suddenly, he found himself here. At this very compound. But it wasn't the present. He saw Towers, tall, but hunched over a hulking, cumbersome figure. A bright blue tarp stretched out underneath him while he donned a milky, yet transparent apron ripe with cut marks and splatters of rose red blood.

"Well let me break it down for you," Towers continued. "The lines are getting a little blurry. The gap between right and wrong is so tight that you can't fit a dolphin dick in there, ya feel me?"

"Towers?" Seller asked, deflecting the especially strange comparison.

"Please Butcher, don't interrupt me. I'm not finished yet."

Interjecting immediately, Seller said, "As much as I do love the dulcet tones of your voice, my skull is on the verge of exploding. So, if you could, please get to the point, or just do what you came to do already." The movie reel pulsing in his mind revealed Towers hacking at the human mess below. Nausea settled into Seller's stomach like an albatross landing over a trip across seas. Dry heaving, he curled up into a fetal position.

"Sounds like the coffee is working..." Towers said as his pitch reached an octave higher.

"How do you mean?" Seller asked as he retched.

"Why do you think the coffee has been so shitty the past few days? Let me just answer that for you. I made the coffee. Guess what I put in it?" Towers asked in giddy anticipation. Seller pulled his gaze away from the stained vinyl tiles and up towards Towers. The man that Seller once knew was morphing into something unfamiliar. Not in physical bulk, but his stature changed; he stood taller, his arms hung lower, and his smile twisted into an unsettling curl. No doubt the man he was looking at was Towers, but the man inside was different. "Morphine," he said impatiently. "It's morphine. Not a lot, just a smidge." A maniacal laugh erupted from his lips. "Just enough to make your mind wander, but apparently you wandered a little too far.

"Ya see, I was gettin' worried you were catching on, so I started planting tiny doses of dope in your coffee. So minute that, sure your coffee would taste like shit, but you would be none the wiser with the awful shit they trough out at the station. But you feel it now, don't you? Slipping into your nervous system, coursing your veins as the dopamine releases. Seeing shit, maybe?"

Seller looked up with a slight eyebrow raised.

"You do, don't you?" Towers said enlightened. He crouched as he peered deeply into Seller. "Tell me, what do you see?"

"I see you," Seller muttered as the dry heaves subsided. "See you for who you have always been, ya sick fuck."

"Oh yeah?" Towers replied, interest piqued. "You got me pegged? Down to the finest detail?"

"Yeah," Seller replied wryly. He chose his next words carefully. His window to avoid being the next exhibit in Towers meat hook art gallery was rapidly closing. "I see you found a new hobby – a hobby including people and hooks. Or maybe it isn't new. Maybe you've been experimenting since you were a wee little tot. I guess that's a little more likely. Started with small animals. Maybe cats? Dogs? Either way. Maybe you've been soiling the bed too. Setting small fires to sheds, maybe even bigger structures. Maybe you've been calling me Butcher sarcastically just to find a way to tell me without telling me that you're a sadistic, man slicing, testicle rearranger-er this whole time. That about right, or am I off the mark?"

"Hah, ding-ding-ding! What do we have for him, Johnny?"

"Hopefully, nothing." Seller said. "Now, why the cocaine and poker table? Doesn't really seem like your style."

"Diversion. That's all. Makes you think about that stinkin' slut that Mr. Rudd had so graciously placed into my murder scene."

"Musta been destiny, from the looks of it and all..."

Towers broke into raucous laughter, booming in his usual way. His sidearm went skyward as he rocked back, and then lurched forward his weapon now rested on his thigh pointing opposite of Seller.

As the moment of opportunity opened, Seller rolled toward his piece, grabbed it with the precision of a frog snatching a fly, and lay on his back as he fired. The shot plunged through Towers cheek and pushed through the back of his skull, dropping him to the floor.

Seller's headache cleared, and he threw off the soreness racking his body as he rose to his feet. Towers attempted raising his weapon and popped off a round, but it wasn't in Seller's vicinity. Seller fired another shot into Towers grip. The gun hopped out of his hand as the blood streamed from the new hole in his palm. He gaped down at his moribund colleague.

Groaning, Towers said, "Well shit. That did... not go the... the way I... I thought it would. Fucken Dr. Phil over here... figured me out." He chuckled as he choked on blood. The choking turned into gargling, and then his chest fell, never to rise again.

Standing in the dark, cold empty hardware store Seller could only rustle up one thought. "Now, look at that fucken mess."

PLIGHT OF THE PITIFUL

I wish I could sing no regrets

And no emotional debt

'Cause as we kissed goodbye, the sun sets

So we are history

Your shadow covers me

The sky above ablaze

That only lovers see

      - "Tears Dry on Their Own" by Amy Winehouse

CONTENT WARNING: REFERENCES TO CHILD ABUSE

CHAPTER ONE

I n Minnesota, you'll find - in between townhouse developments, single family homes, and commercial America - pockets of trailer parks teeming with an unfortunate sort of peoples. Some are down on their luck, some prefer a simpler, inexpensive lifestyle, and others are cursed from the start, just destined to lose. Flea belonged to the latter. The runt of the litter. The last of five boys. In order they went Brick, Stone, the twins Mason and Rock, and lastly Flea.

Life for poor Flea was one with body aches and tears. He was the constant source of humiliation acting as the family punching bag. His face lumpy from the countless times his brothers mashed their fists into him, and body swollen from the broom whacks, whirling batteries, and resin action figures thrust into his sides. One time, the twins found a baseball in the road and took turns tossing fastballs into Flea's guts. His lips were often split, and the top of his head resembled a squeezed together clump of clay complete with an assortment of unnatural bumps and pocks and scores. Being on the precipice of puberty was tough enough on its own, he didn't need the extra growing pains.

Out of shape and apathetic, Flea's mother let the brothers do their damage. Instead of issuing any kind of discipline or regimenting a sort of structure, she stayed laying in a broken recliner that groaned under her weight, wearing a night gown that strained at every seam, begging for space.

A pair of crutches stood up leaning against the wall, far enough to force her to reach, but close enough for her to roll a bit and grope the crutches by her fingertips and spin them into grip. She was watching daytime soap operas and guzzling bargain brand soda. Her teeth were wrought with cavities, streaking from yellow to brown, from tooth to tooth, like a grading scale, and the stench of her breath was like fire scorching any and every living thing in its path.

"Flea, you gaht damn piece of shit! Come 'eer!" Not only was she all things below vile in appearance, she had the temperament to match. She didn't need to be roused into escalation. It was a natural disposition. She added, "Git over 'eer and grab my Coke."

"But Ma, yer right there..." The dejected tone of his voice was coupled with the speed of a sloth's crawl.

Shifting in her seat, the chair protested in a series of groans. His mom reached for a pop can from the side table, crumpled it like scratch paper and hurled it at Flea. The empty can whiffled in the air and bounced off his chest. "Don't talk back! You better shut yer damn mouth and git over 'eer and get it, you lazy sunnuva bitch!" she demanded ironically. Her jowls jiggled and produced a gargle with whatever saliva she stored in her fat neck pockets, while the weight of her chest rattled her lungs.

"But ma, yer talkin' bad about yer-self."

Whirring like a boomerang, the television remote shattered against his forehead casting plastic pieces in every direction. The batteries of the thing landed at his toes. "Gaht dammit! Look what you made me do! Now imma hafta buy a new remote cuz of yer dumb ass," she sneered at him. One that sent his stomach into square knots. The kind with ropes that burned as they cinched tighter and coiled over ends until they were drawn taut with each new careless word that tripped out of her piss-stained mouth. Her raucous screams turned into low guttural growls, "Now git 'eer and git me that Coke. And if you say one more word, I'll beat you with my crutch."

Agreeing was easier, and he realized he should not have said a word in the first place. Saved him trouble that way. A new lump formed on his forehead. He rubbed it while it throbbed. But Flea was born to learn the hard way, even if that meant learning it repeatedly.

With droopy shoulders and slouched posture, he slunk over to get the soda she requested. *Slap.* His mother whacked him for good measure. He yelped in pain and handed the warm can of soda and slithered out of there like a snake with his tail caught on fire. She cackled in her recliner with her neck and arm fat shaking violently, enough to make the most seasoned seamen sick, while another spring in her seat gave way sinking another inch into the chair which meant it would require a greater effort to pry that 400-pound mass from her posterior.

Flea ran off with tears in his eyes and hurt in his stomach. He weaved through the messy mobile home, and slipped into his cramped bedroom, also known as Brick's closet. Comfort did not come easy to Flea. Everywhere in life he was not wanted, and frankly felt often he would be better off dead. However, he lacked the courage to even think of more than just not existing. So, he went on wasting away in the dark recesses of a sixteen-square foot room, which he found to be a warm blanket to keeping him cozy in a volatile environment. Being blindfolded from the outside world was the only remedy to a jackhammer heart. When he hyperventilated, he could feel the knots in his stomach slip and loosen, aching still, but relieved all the while. It would mean nothing. Anytime Flea felt like life was about to become manageable, Brick happened. The eldest, the worst. Brick aggressively masturbated into a dirty washcloth, one he dubbed the *nut-rag*, every afternoon, and shoved it in Flea's face. Then he'd grind the thing up Flea's forehead and scour it back down to the chin as if he were sanding the rough edges of a pinewood derby car.

Everyone hated him, without any good reason. The kids at school hated him because he dressed in nothing but hand-me-down muscle shirts, stained enough to make a person wonder which color it started out as, and smelled like dog waste baking under the noon-high sun. They laughed at him when he tried to read aloud, stuttering on every word, and if he mispronounced one of them, the class would give him hell, whooping and hollering until he sank so lowly in his desk that he might have become one with it. They, and even his teachers, took turns teasing him at the front of the classroom calling him a dirty, worthless hillbilly. The words meant nothing, but the hate behind it was caustic, stuck to his bones.

His father was unimportant. He left after he was conceived as he couldn't handle, "another piece of shit runnin' 'round the house." As we already know, his brothers were a wealthy source of needling pain. And clearly, his mother thought well enough to call him Flea, so there's that. In fact, the only person in the entire loathsome globe that gave a damn about Flea was the girl who lived a few trailer-park blocks across the way. Tina.

Outside of the beautiful, bouncy blonde curls, Tina did not offer much else to look at. She had round cheeks, a button nose, with rows of teeth as synchronously gapped as a cogwheel. Her body was as lumpy as Flea's face. Chicken skin ran rampant along her arms and legs. Despite her overall reproachful appearance, she was darling and precious, always sensitive to the plight of the pitiful. She was drawn to the pain in Flea's eyes. Every time he suffered another blow, be it from words or of the physical sort, another bit of her heart would fracture and tumble away, never to return. Flea didn't know she cared so much on the account of him being suffocated by his own misery. He did not have the time or capacity to recognize anyone else.

That was until one day, Flea had been beaten to a pulp by a few of his brothers out in the street because he had tried to read a comic book. The dialogue and exposition boxes were far too small, and he could hardly read as it was, but he liked the pictures and picked up context clues in each frame. Their perfect form of derision always began with "Nerd" and "Faggot" and other unkind terms. From there, they went to ripping the comic book out of his hands and shredding it from cover to cover. After they tore up his comic book and stripped his pleasure bare, they dragged him by his arms and legs, tossed him into the narrow street in front of their home, and rained down flurries of punches and kicks and spat on him until he balled up in pain and cried in embarrassment. The burning, black tar singed the fine, prepubescent hair of his arms, neck, and legs adding to the cascade of aromatic stench of unbathed skin, iron, and despair. Flea sat there motionless as tears streamed his face. He was fortunate enough that his brothers found a cat running down the street - another thing to torture – so he curled up in a centipede-ball and tended to the pain all about him.

A cool hand soothed his scrawny, pipe arms. There was a power to the touch, but it was merciful and gracious, not the kind coupled with knuckled edges or brought down with malice. Not even the occasional brush ups were this soft. This was different. It was sweet. It was tender. It was pleasant. For a moment, the world ceased to move. He shoved the sun light aside with an urging hand as Tina shifted into Flea's frame of vision. "Hi Flea," her voice was melodic. Dulcet. "That is your name, isn't it? Flea?"

"Umm, yeah," Flea answered dizzily. Yup it is."

Tina pulled his gaze and crashed into contact with her watery blue eyes. "They are so awful to you. Do they really treat you like that all the time?"

Her voice played in his ears like the golden strings of a harpsichord, strummed by angelic fingers, each note playing with a willful intention to heal his aching heart. "Yup. They're like that alla the time. They always been like that." There weren't words Flea could form that could describe his confusion. All the looks he ever received were either those of jagged-toothed snarls and unhinged jaws guffawing over his misfortune and misery. She was different. She was kind. She was listening. Her tight-lipped smile produced the cutest crease between her mouth's curled edges and her round cheeks. His body throbbed, but his heart pounded happily. "You must be an angel come down to save me. Yer an angel, aren't you?" He asked, slack-jawed and dizzy. Truth was, he believed it. Sure as the rising sun brings heat to a cool and dark Earth, he was fixed on an angel.

She giggled lightly and politely said no. Tina was used to the worst kind of people. The trailer park teemed with the ill-tempered, nefarious, and the like. Being a too-sweet, portly, and somewhat dim-witted girl, she was subjected to the most deplorable sort of people. Her father was just as rotten. Whenever dad had a hard day with the paper route, he'd come back and smack her mom, and Tina would walk in and would ask, with eyes so bright and innocent, what Mom had done to deserve the abuse. He'd haul another backhand off her round, rosy cheeks and tell her to mind her business. She would always well up but would never cry. And there were those days he was particularly nasty.

There was a place in Tina's heart that fought the hurt she harbored with delightful thoughts; deflecting the insidious and replacing them with the sweetness of ice cream and butterflies. That usually did the trick.

Flea was the first boy she had seen being treated unfairly. In fact, he was the only other human being she witnessed suffering the very same throes she had. No one loved her the way she ought to have been loved. Just like Flea. Neither of them deserved the trouble they endured.

From then on, they forged a pact and it was love like instant coffee; it wasn't pretty, and it was hard on the stomach, but to them it was beautiful, and it didn't matter what other people thought. They had each other and that would suffice.

Routinely, Flea ran away from home. His mother was oblivious and too sunken into her ragged recliner to call the cops or to really do anything. He would always come back home after a few days. Fortunately, most of the time his mother wouldn't notice he was even gone. Normally not being cared enough about to even be registered as missing would hurt Flea, but now it gave him the freedom to do what he pleased with Tina by his side.

The brood of brothers still picked on him like hell. They'd sling barbs about Tina like, "Hey Flea! I don't think that hog is street legal! They'll probably lock you away for squealing down the road with ham and a side of bacon." For the gruesome and twisted bunch they were, they found clever ways to hurt Flea. The only problem was Flea didn't care what they thought or said anymore. He'd become numb to their words and simply shrug them off with his measly shoulders and run off to her house. They didn't like that much so instead of words, they rained down rocks as he pedaled away.

Whenever the two would meet, she would be waiting outside, smile all aglow, and peck Flea on the cheek and hop on the metal pegs. The bike would sink, the spokes would groan, and Flea would disappear into the thin yellow line in the sky. Eventually they'd cut into an overgrown trail, indiscreet enough that only they would know exactly where to go. Just a couple hundred meters deep into the vegetation was a makeshift fort with particle board fashioned together with long-tooth staples, propped up against a dying oak tree with wiry branches stretched out like whiskers of a bedraggled cat.

Inside they would cuddle and kiss and revel in the ardor of their love for one another. They thought about engaging in sex, even discussed it some, but both lacked the rudimentary understanding of the act and had no clue what to where to begin had they gotten that far. They were content in each other's presence and left sex for the rest of the world to figure out.

That was until Flea's brothers followed him and Tina one day to their private place in the woods. On that fateful day, Flea took his usual route out to Tina's home and absconded to their favorite place. The brothers trailed behind close enough to keep visibility on Flea and Tina, but at a careful distance where their sinister snickers and crude remarks were deaf upon the young lovers' ears.

For two miles, they trekked on that hot and steamy day with the black tar screaming, and the telephone lines humming the Flight of the Bumblebees, and not for one second did Flea and Tina bother to look back. They made their usual turn into the woods. A few minutes later the brothers did the same. Lurking slowly behind they kept their sight on Tina's bright and beaming yellow sundress. You could see it even through the density of trees and poison ivy. The brothers watched the deeply-in-love lovebirds slip into their makeshift fort. They remained concealed behind shrubberies and crossed-over trees. Slinking along like silent assassins, they moved with purpose as their tiptoes across the sprouts of grass and packed dirt. One by one, they broke around the fort in a ring.

Brick mouthed a countdown from 5...

4...

3...

2...

1...

"Here Piggy, Piggy, Piggy!" Brick belted as his pack of wild dogs engaged. The ruckus stirred Flea and Tina. From ass to feet, they moved quickly as possible. It did not matter. The brothers converged swiftly, shoving them both to the ground, tearing the ramshackle fort, board-by-board with ease. Clawing madly and laughing maniacally, they tossed each plank carelessly, some hitting the pair, some landing just short of their limbs.

Flea and Tina laid on their sides holding each other's hands with their eyes screwed shut. Before the shack had been deconstructed entirely, Brick was sure to hand each of the cackling brothers a board. One brother shouted in a nasally voice, "I love you, Tina!" The rest hollered and whooped, like crazed chimpanzees, laughing and mimicking each other as they raged on slamming boards rife with long-legged staples digging into Flea's and Tina's skin.

For another two minutes, the brothers hung around like the funk of roadkill congratulating each other for the mess they made. They spit on them, threw rocks and fort debris on them. Brick strutted around them, circling like an impatient buzzard, and shot snot-rockets over them. He snickered as he gestured jerking-off. Brick looked to his brothers and they howled in approval. "Look here Flea," Brick sucked through his teeth, rubbing the scum off his unbrushed rows of teeth one-by-one. "You can trrrryyyyy and be happy being with a pig who feeds off yer sloppy little knobby, but the sad, sad truth of yer life is yer just gonna be the same weaselly piece of shit who gets beat on by his ma and brothers. The same scrawny sunnuva-bitch who sleeps in *my* fuckin' closet. A silly little faggot who washes his grimy face with *my nut-rag*!"

Brick scoured Flea's eyes, who wouldn't bother to jerk his head upwards to give him the satisfaction of a pleading look. For the last show of dominance, Brick snatched up Flea's bicycle with a single arm and flipped it onto his youngest brother. Flea caught a metal peg to the groin. The pang crashed into him like a rogue wave. He fought the urge to cry by swallowing rapidly and ducking his head into his chest.

Brick knelt on Flea's wrist and spat into his ear as he whispered, "See you back in the fucking closet, fag. I'll have my nut-rag hot, *wet* and ready."

None of this hurt more than their careless tongues hurling insults of their love for each other. After the fun was done, the brothers disengaged, cackled a little more, and peeled out of the woods with upturned middle fingers.

The two young lovers were battered and beaten, bruised from heel to forehead with incessant cuts smothered in dirt here and there. They cried and groaned in agony together as they rolled inwards and were face-to-face. Flea's eyes were cinched tight as he struggled to find which part of his body hurt most. Instead he reached out to comfort Tina who writhed in pain. They huddled closer as Flea opened his eyes and surveyed Tina with a watery eye. When Tina came to, Flea noticed that the twinkle in her eye, that he admired and adored so much, was gone. She was officially broken, and he could do nothing to help. No amount of "I love you" could restore the gleam in her eye and Flea felt a healthy chunk of his heart sever and tumble away.

CHAPTER TWO

Tina sat gaping emptily at the plate of food in front of her. She stirred a serving of peas and carrots, the fork tines combing with no direction. A small part of her was separating the two vegetables, but it was purposeless. The entire plate of food was pointless. She was only going to stare at it until it was time to return to class.

The cafeteria was abuzz with prepubescent chatter – teenagers griping about personal matters. A group of boys talked about how their parents wouldn't allow them to play video games for more than two hours at a time. A group of girls were upset about how their parents asked to have their door propped open when they had boys in their room. Another group gossiped about sex and who was doing 'it'. She was exhausted and could do away with any of the middle school politics.

Flea rushed over to sit next to Tina while his busted-up sneakers flapped revealing his sockless feet, his toes acting like a tongue. He plopped down next to her and stretched his arm out over her shoulders to hug her sideways. She flinched.

"What's the matter?" Flea asked

"Nothing," She answered coldly.

"I reckon that ain't true. You been a little off today. I don't mean that rude-like, it's just been weird that's all."

A shiver drove up her spine and set her flesh rippling with goosebumps. Flea leaned in a little closer.

"You can tell me, ya know? You can trust me. I love you."

"He..." she balked. Her elbows were planted on the table, her fingers bloomed from her palms and clutched together as if she were praying. Pain swelled in her chest. Overwhelming pressure threatened to crack ribs and consume her neck and shoulders. Tears burned as they bubbled to the surface. She trembled as she drew her arms in and reached to cover her face, her hands failing to catch the already falling droplets. She mumbled as she spoke, "He touched me."

Red with rage Flea asked, but knew anyway, "Who touched you?" He balled up his puny fists and pumped them like he was milking a cow. It wasn't news that Tina's father was getting drunker and meaner as each day passed. Beating her mother wasn't enough and braying insults and cutting remarks wasn't doing the job. The inflicted pain wasn't paying the penance, so he dug deeper to right his wrongs. Flea recalled Tina telling him that her father, had inappropriately touched her chest. "It was him again, wuddn't it?"

Her round face scrunched up like she bit into a lemon and nodded. She tried to speak, but she couldn't. All day the memory of last night's wrongful touching was eating her alive. Flashes of his hands crawling all over her made her convulse and wince. Flea sat there watching on as Tina broke all the way down.

"I'mma kill em'."

Tina did not respond. Flea was always bundled up with some fierce anger in his heart which led him to all sorts of bumbling threats. His ability to harm was that of a fly. He'd puke on someone's boots out of sheer anxiety before he could work up the nerve to raise a fist and strike a person. This was normally followed by Tina utilizing comforting words to bring him back down to earth. 'Don't be silly' was the most common retort, and every time there would be a retort, but this time she said nothing. She cocked her head to look at him; the pools of blue stunned Flea and floored him with a single nod.

The color drained from Flea's face. Panic filled in. The buzzing fluorescent lights above casted a waxy complexion over every uneven ridge and bump of what was Flea's face. Stuttering, he asked, "Ya... ya... ya mean..."

Without blinking, she coldly bobbed her head again. Insidious thoughts flared up. Her golden gates of positivity placed high on alabaster clouds had decayed and crumbled to earth. Every bad memory was a cancer metastasizing from her weakened heart. Tina wanted nothing more in the world than to have Daddy go away. Forever.

Flea's guts twisted into an unfamiliar square knot. This was a shock to the system. A wave of unclean, obscure ripping tides, relentlessly splashing his face. Sure, he'd toss out an empty threat, but that was what they were. Empty as the schoolyard bullies. Empty as Flea's brothers and mother. Empty as Tina's child molesting father. No, her father was an exception. His soul was a shade of black that rested in the darkest corners of a prison cell. Shadows revolving around a raging fire; casted from demons dancing to a devil tune. His soul was a black hole; a massive raven hand collecting all matter, leaving nothing to chance, nothing to remain, but a longing for existence had it not been effaced by a lurking, all-consuming evil. Flea could not consider him human.

A few days passed. Tina grew despondent. The choppy waters in her eyes calmed into a swim-less blue. What words she had to say were sealed between her thin lips. Not even Flea was blessed with her voice. Until one day after school.

Since the day they were flogged in their happy place, they never returned to the site. Too much sorrow had been buried in the grounds there. Instead they hung around the school yard, tucked away on the back-corner lot, far from plain view of the street to stay hidden from Flea's rotten brothers.

"We must get on with it," her voice burning with purpose. Flea may not have been smart, but he knew. No clue or context was needed.

"How should we do it?" he asked. He regretted it too. For days, he hoped that she would have forgotten his willingness to aide in a violent crime. Was her father a terrible person? Yes, but that didn't help his squelching stomach from tightening and twisting into a fierce square knot. Besides, he didn't have the brains to figure out how to even broach the topic of how to kill someone. They needed an architect. They needed a blueprint. What they needed was someone who knew what they were doing.

"Very carefully," she chewed on her bottom lip. Tina had spent the past few days crafting a plan that was destined to not fail. "My mom goes to Bingo every Thursday. She's gone from six at night until about eight. He," referring to her dad, "is black out drunk by six fifteen. We take his gun from the bedroom drawer and blast him in his *fucking* face."

The anger in her eyes roared like gasoline flames, and Flea sat there gaping dumbfounded as she uttered the harshest word imaginable. Sure, he heard it from the usual suspects, Brick and his brutish crew, his mother's melding body to the rickety chair, even from the snarky children in his class, but not from her. He stood there frozen.

"Now, it's important that you follow my every word. We'll be working in a tight window, and we can't mess-up even once - cuz if you do, we'll be in a whole heap-a-trouble. Once you leave, I'll call the cops and say we were robbed and give them a description of your older brother. Brick, right?"

A lump formed in Flea's throat as he answered, "Well, I mean... yeah. That's his name. But why would we do that?"

"Flea, need I remind you what that sack of shit has done to you? What *he,* and your brothers, did to us when all we ever wanted to be was to just be alone? His afternoon *rituals*?"

He knew perfectly well what she meant by Brick's 'afternoon *rituals.* "No, you needn't remind me, but..."

"No buts, Flea. We are doing this. Your brothers are assholes, with Brick being 'specially evil. They can no longer get away with doing the dirty stuff they do. They deserve what's coming to em and you should be happy that we're the ones doin' it'."

Flea nodded. She was right. It made sense. He was going to go along with anything she said, so if she believed in what she was saying, then he'd toe the line.

"So, we are in agreement?"

"Yes. But how could I even do it, Tina."

"You'll have to get strong Flea. I'll be there with you every step of the way."

Thursday swooped in like a barn owl plucking an unsuspecting mouse from a grassy field. Flea trembled in his classroom seat, gripped by the sudden arrival of *the* day. The steel legs clanged against the vinyl tiled floor. His muscle shirt soaked in sweat. His third period teacher asked if he was ok. Flea said he was. The teacher thought otherwise. The rest of the school day, Flea laid in a barely padded mattress in the back corner of the nurse's office where gray slabs of concrete walls stole the breath from his lungs. He closed his eyes to rest, but he would never know that comfort again.

The final school bell rang. Kids poured out of every door and filled into the streets. As the flow died down, Flea hobbled out, hunched over with his guts grouped together in his hands. Every step was a threat to vomit. He took his time walking down the steps and met Tina in their new usual spot.

"You ready?"

"I don't know, Tina. I've got them square knots in mah stomach and they're tight."

"Flea," she said sternly. "This is it. The time is now. Don't you hate him just as much as I do?"

"Yeah, but..."

"No buts, Flea," it had become Tina's mantra for his ambivalence. "This is the right thing to do. This world is better off without him. He is pond scum. He is a monster. If we do this, the world will thank us. We need to take this into our own hands. It's the right thing to do."

Pain bled through her fiery veil. Anger was a thin veneer she wore, but Flea could see through that, and hated that she didn't have the resolve to keep her demons at bay. His mind flooded with hatred for the man who destroyed her innocence. That man would have to pay, and Flea was going to collect the debt. He nodded, this time with less trepidation.

CHAPTER THREE

Night fall approached. Tina and Flea hung around outside and peered through the window while her father pounded another beer; then switched to a bottle of whiskey and set it on the side table. He twisted the cap, tipped it back, and shuddered as the liquor swirled down his throat.

Tina gazed over at her father's alarm clock. 6:10 glowed in red, segmented numbers on the black background. She looked over at Flea. He looked focused. More than ever. This made her happy.

The look on Tina's father's face was the queue. His eyelids swung shut like the vault door on a bank safe. Slowly but surely, they pushed and pushed and with a final flurry of flutters the eyelids fell entirely. Flea snapped to his feet causing the fallen leaves beneath him to rustle. Tina grabbed his wrist and wrenched him down. Her father shook in his chair and opened his eyes. The two crouched under the window out of plain sight. They rose to the edge of the window and peeked over the threshold. He was out again.

"You have to wait 'til he shakes a bit," She whispered. "Then you know he is out like a light."

Sure enough, the sleep jolted throughout his body causing the nerves to tug at his skin. After his arms and legs jumped, the extremities falling back into position, his hand rolled off to the side. His head lolled back, and his jaw sagged revealing the front row of teeth – they shoved out like the first half of a bear trap. He choked on breath and exhaled a snore which was the final indicator he was incapacitated.

"Now!" Tina sharply exhaled.

The two sidled along the home and entered through the back door. They crept heel-toe heel-toe, on the linoleum floor until they reached the forgiving cushion of the carpeted bedroom where the gun was stashed in the bedroom drawer, just as Tina had called it.

"Listen to me," Tina said quietly. "I want you to grab that bottle of whiskey he's got set in front of him and smack him in the face, so he wakes up. But keep the gun aimed on him so he doesn't try to do something stupid. I have something I want to say to him first before you blast a hole between his eyes."

Flea nodded. He said nothing. He was afraid if he had said anything the courage of following through with the plan would have leapt out with the words leading the way.

Through the narrow hallway they walked determinedly and stood before her father sleeping so warmly unaware of what hell was to come. Tina snatched the bottle of whiskey from the side table and handed it to Flea. He took it from her hand and awaited the next block of instruction. She stared directly at Flea, leaned her head over towards her father and raised her brows with a face inferring, 'Do I need to do everything for you?'

The square knots tightened. They never left. They constricted, now burning. Flea looked listless, and Tina saw it drawn all over his face.

139

This was the moment. It was time. He needed the push, and she was going to deliver. She bubbled and shouted, "Do it!"

Her father startled out of sleep and barely into consciousness. Flea trusted instinct would kick in, but it didn't. Something kept the head and the heart separate. No matter what his mind wanted him to do, the body would not respond. He was losing time, and this disconnect swallowed each tick-tock like Tic-Tacs. All he could do was point the gun in his direction and tell him not to move, but his arm hung slack with the bottle barely gripped in his fingertips. Tina's father shot to his feet and covered ground rapidly as he made his way towards Flea. Tina erupted with cries, while her father boomed with threats, and none of it mattered as it all washed together in a bleary moment and with a blink, everything went black for Flea.

When he snapped back to it the gun was flopping in his right hand like a fish gasping for air. The bottle in his other hand gripping the neck as what used to be the base was now jagged glass jutting out like shark teeth. Tina's father was plastered back on his chair bleeding and crying.

"What do you want from me?"

"I want you to apologize." Tina spoke calmly, but resolutely.

"For what?"

Her head whipped in disbelief as she roared, "FOR WHAT? You can't be that dense. I've always thought you were a *fucking* idiot, but I didn't think you were blind. Let's hope you're not deaf, because I'm going to spell it out for you, so there isn't any confusion. For starters, hitting mom when she didn't deserve it. She does everything. She does your laundry, feeds you, and cleans the puke from your pants when you wake up from being a *pathetic – useless – fucking* drunk. She would probably wipe your ass if you asked her. But you," she rose a crooked finger and pointed at him, "you treat her like a half-drowned rat trying to find a place in the world less stinky and rotten than this *fucking* hellhole. Hit him again Flea!"

Without a word, Flea slapped him with the bottle scoring another three gouges into the space between his cheekbone and jaw blood surging from the wounds.

"For hitting me," she continued with spit congregating at the corners of her lips, "when *I* didn't deserve it. All I wanted to do is try to be sweet and kind and do what is good and true, and apparently that just wasn't good enough for you. You made me this way. Tortured and destroyed. You'd rather not hear me or not see me, unless you want to *fucking* touch me, you sick *fuck!*" A bulging vein streaked her forehead Another two veins coursed her neck. She was hardly coming up for air. Spittle leapt from her lips as gusts of breath broke free. "Oh yeah, that too... For touching me and sticking your filthy little thing in me when *I didn't deserve it!* Is that clear enough for you? Do you get the *fucking* picture? *You fucking pervert?*"

"I'm sorry, Tina. Tina – Tina, I'm so sorry. I love you. I promise to never touch you or your mom again. I never meant to hurt you. I – I – I just can't help it."

"You can't help it?" tongues of flames seemingly reaching out from her eyes, "You can't help being a *fucking pervert?* Maybe you can't help yourself. So, you know what, *we* will help you. Hell, we'll help ourselves." She signaled to Flea with her fingers in the form of a gun.

He raised the gun and trained the sights in between her father's eyes.

"Wait, listen. Flea, right? Yeah, Flea. Please don't do this. You'll go to jail for the rest of your life and your life will be ruined."

"Be *strong* Flea, don't listen to him." Tina encouraged him.

"Please, come on. You don't want your life to be ruined do ya?"

Flea looked coldly into Tina's father's eyes and said nothing. His thumb climbed up the hammer and peeled it back. He never had done it before, but the movies made it seem so easy. His hand pulsed as he choked the pistol grip. He made a crook in his forefinger and slid it into the trigger well. A deep breath came in like a rising tide and came out washing up on shore – the breath stopping as it quietly reached its peak.

He winced as the gun cracked. The barrel hardly kicked. The crash rang in his ears, his sight jarred. He fixed his feet into shoulder-width position, his knees wobbled. His arms shot out to grab someone, but nothing was there. He damn near toppled over he was so dizzy.

Being scared he had missed pulled him from the brief break in focus. He shook off the noise and looked up at Tina's father. A quarter-sized hole interrupted the space between the bridge of her father's nose to where his hairline would have been had he not been balding. From it, blood oozed down his mouth and dribbled to his chest. Splotches of blood casted behind the dead man. Flea stood in shock, his mouth dry and wide open.

"Go!" Tina shouted. "Leave now! I'm calling the cops. Take the bottle with you, put it in the bag. And the gun, keep that. We might need it later." Flea had stolen Brick's book bag before leaving for school per Tina's instruction. He continued her to-do list and stormed out of the house. After running around to the backyard, he pedaled into the trees slipping into the black expanse of the night.

Flea rolled into the driveway of his home several minutes later. His brothers were gone, and his morbidly obese mother conducted a cacophony of snores bellowing from her deviated septum blasting out of her flaring nostrils. He grabbed a towel from the linen closet and opened Brick's bag. He wrapped the towel around the handle of the bottle and returned it, then wiped down the rest of the bag, just like Tina had said to. He didn't know why, he was just following orders, but he thought well enough to keep the towel with him. He crept out of the house with a single creak groaning from the door hinge, but his mother was too occupied with being fat and lazy.

The sky was a black ceiling with moisture sucked from the ground to Flea's lips that he could drink in every drop. Down the street he could hear his brothers clamoring among the buzz of telephone lines invading his eardrums. He hopped back on the bike and tore down the road and back into the woods where he would wash up in a creek nearby.

He scrubbed the blood off his arms and formed his feeble hands into cups and splashed his face, clearing it from any crusted blood. The water dribbled to his neck and ran to his shirt. His stomach was empty. He couldn't remember when he last ate, but the way his arms and body trembled he had known it had been too long ago. Thing was, he couldn't eat if he tried. He was weak in strength and fear. He curled into a ball and heaved until he could heave no more. He grew pale and cold. Exhaustion soon followed and made himself a home in the little patch of dirt. The creek's current crashed against rocks and spilled up the sides of the bank. Even though he could not be comfortable, the song of the creek soothed him enough to lull him to sleep. There he spent the night with the wet earth and brisk air.

CHAPTER FOUR

T he sun sucker-punched him. A tingling sensation coursed his body, and he was reminded by his stomach's grumbling protest that it required sustainment. For a moment, he had forgotten everything. His mind flowed with a purity of pristine blue waters, sparkling in the sun. The whole event was blotted from his memory. There was no murder, there was no framing, there was no running. He had been free from the crimes he committed. At least for a moment. It wasn't until then he looked down and saw the creek flowing, the remains of bile he had spilled on the bank, and the steel gray pistol lodged between his pants and belt buckle. To Flea's surprise, the pistol had still been on fire. So, he thumbed the pin to safe. Then, Tina's father's face with a hole in his head rushed into memory. With that came the surging punches of everything. He broke into frantic breaths and hopped to his feet. He brushed the dirt and ants from his pocked face and wheeled back home.

The time was eight o'clock when he busted down the door open of the double wide. He swung his arms in a militant manner, *front-to-*

rear – front-to-rear, as he marched and suddenly slid into a stop. His massive mother was on her feet. A sight to behold. One he hadn't seen in years. She was hunched over the kitchen counter, with a can of pop and her head buried in her tear-soaked hands.

"Flea, where the hell you been?" she lashed out, hardly drawing her head up to speak.

"Ma... is everything ok?" He sounded concerned as if he had no reason why she would be distraught.

"No! No, Flea. Nothing is ok. They took Brick. They took him!"

"They? Who? Took him where?"

"The cops! They took him to jail you dumb ass. They say he killed Mr. Tramper."

His sore guts sunk. The noise around him washed away and his vision narrowed. He didn't think the fallout would happen so rapidly. He figured he could say something to him. Maybe issue an apology. He hated his brothers, but he didn't want to hurt them. Then he was swarmed with flashbacks of the night prior. The portions where he blacked out materialized. The jigsaw puzzle pieced together as he drifted into the blackness of his memory. Then the bottle of whiskey in his hand came together in frame. He was swinging it back and he brought it down like a haymaker screaming from hell. Every bit of glass exploded like shrapnel from Mr. Tramper's forehead at half speed. He caught the light refracting from every shard. Each glint took their turns shining like diamonds in his eyes. He took the time to follow them as they moved so slow, almost as if he was basking in the shower of glass, that they might have even been still. Then, the view was shot from the corner as if security had monitored the entire situation. He was looking at himself. The speed picked back up and in the matter of seconds Flea stood aiming the deadly pistol, his finger wrapped snuggly 'round the trigger, coiling until he pulled all the way back, clicking. Just before impact was made, the frame slowed so you could see every spin of the spent round. Mr. Tramper's face caught the bullet like a strong-armed pass, tossing the rest of him backwards in a graceless dance. His body went slack and crashed into the recliner with reckless abandon. Then the frame speed picked up. And then again faster. *Hit - Blast.* And faster. *Hit- Blast.* And even faster, so fast that the memory was now on loop and each time he fired the gun Flea noticed he was becoming less and less afraid of the blast. He craned his head around and gazed lovingly at Tina. She had already been looking fondly at him. Their connection was eternally forged. Nothing would stand between him and her. He needed to get strong, and this was it. This was the power he was searching for, and now it burned down deep within him and nestled into a nook in his heart.

"Snap the hell out of it, boy!" The back of his mom's hand came hard and fast, dragging her knuckles across his cheek bone with proper follow thru. She drew the hand back up, for seconds, and came down fast. Except this time, no face was there.

"No more mama," Flea stood as tall and mighty as his scrawny little body could, his cheek rosy from the strike, but his hands remained at his side. Even though it stung, he didn't want to show he had been hurt. She didn't need that satisfaction. "You been mean to me fer far too long. I'm sorry bout Brick, but you ain't needin' to hit me no more. I don't deserve it!"

Another swat came down, but Flea wasn't prepared. His cheek rippled from the contact and cut the insides of his mouth with his jagged teeth. "Shut yer filthy mouth, little boy! When I'm talking, you just need to shut yer ass up and listen to me. I think you got something to do with what happened last night. Brick said he ain't seen his bag all day yesterday and alla sudden a man ends up dead. Did you have Brick's bag? Where were you last night, you whiny little stink?"

The ropes in his stomach started to wrap around and bind up into one of those square knots, but he took a deep breath. He could feel the panic subside. He was getting good at this. "It don't matter where I was, Mama, and no I ain't have his bag yesterday neither. You sound crazy, Ma. Jus' listen to yerself."

"Why you little..." Her arms flailed out in an attempt to grab Flea, but he had already side-stepped out of her range. He grabbed a banana quick, his growling bell reminding him just how hungry he was and thundered out of the double wide and slammed the storm door behind him as his mom trailed off shouting accusations and blubbering about her eldest son. He wasn't sure what he was going to do now, having done what he had done, but he knew he had to foster similar appearances. However, he knew things were going to be different now. Flea was emboldened. Disposing of Tina's father was hard, but after purging last evening and finally stepping up to his god-awful mother and lying to her face, the change had come.

He burned rubber and smashed the banana into his mouth. He was at the school in no time. Late wasn't unusual for Flea, so he delayed getting to class just so he could peek into Tina's classroom. Except she wasn't there. He forgot. She told him she would stay home on 'the account of her father being murdered and all', but she asked him to skip as well and meet her at her home.

The bell rang, and teenagers flooded from their respective classrooms. Before Flea could slip away from the crowd, every student stopped and stared. Throttled by the quietude of the usual bustling and boisterous hallways, Flea flinched. This created a wave of flinching amongst the crowd mixed in with a note of panic.

"Your brother is a murderer!" A voice shrieked from somewhere in the pool of people. "I bet yer just like him!"

Never in his life had power been so presently in his hands. Instead of the same old square knot forming in his stomach, he stood up straight, shoulders back, chest puffed out, and screamed, "To hell with all of ya! None of ya are worth a good Goddamn! Not even on a Sunday!" The crowd sat stunned with jaws dropped from front-to-back.

This was for every time some kid hurled a hurtful word, a barb that would sting far past the moment. For every time a teacher bristled when he tried, and every moment he was put down by random passersby. He felt every scar in him well up and now he was above them all and had them gripped by the balls.

"You all can stand there and judge me if ya like, but ya need to know yer not better than me. Sure, you seem nicer with yer pretty hair and clothes, but inside yer rotten. Yer rotten like them apples fallen off the tree. Jus' like them people who say they mean well but lie between their teeth. Yer mouths are full of garbage and everything you say is trash jus' pourin' out like it's been raided by raccoons. You can find someone else to pick fights with, cuz Flea ain't havin' it no-more." And with his third-person parting shot to the crowd he barged through the sea of students which then eventually opened up. His confidence climbed to new heights as he pushed open the school doors. He turned around and flipped both middle fingers up to the sky and scaled backwards down the stairs. Flea reveled in his newfound courage.

Tina sat with her arms folded, head down, trying to wring some tears out of those emotionless eyes. Her mom heaved and sobbed as she spoke with the detective. The detective came back to ask questions because Brick killing Mr. Tramper, aside from the evidence directly connecting him there, didn't make sense, and the gun still hadn't been found. He had asked if Mr. Tramper kept any guns in the home, but to Tina's surprise her mother knew nothing of the pistol he had stashed in the drawer next to his side of the bed. After he gently pressed her for information, she leaned into him and cried. "Why would some awful little teenager take him from us?" All the detective could offer was a generic condolence and a promise to ensure justice be served. He recorded the information she gave, passed her and Tina a card just in case they hear anything else, and made his way back to the station. Flea pulled in shortly after he pulled out. Tina's mother went inside.

"Who was that?" He asked Tina.

Tina picked her head up and handed him the card.

"I can't read this. What's it say?"

Her eyes rolled and then stared coldly at Flea. "His name is Detective Seller. It doesn't matter who he is anyway. Where were you? I thought I told you to come here right away in the morning." Flea started to explain, but she interrupted, "It doesn't matter."

"What's the plan then, Tina?"

"Don't call me that."

"Don't call you what? Tina?"

"Yes, I'm done with that name." She sucked up her gut and stood proud. She poked her head around and glanced at the windows. She could see her mom was keeping herself from crying by doing dishes in the kitchen. "My stupid parents gave me that name and I can't stand hearing my father using it in my head anymore. *Tina this* - *Tina that* - It makes me want to chop off all my hair."

Flea felt uncomfortable. "Do you regret what happened last night?"

"Hell no!" She stood on the top step peering down at Flea. "That bastard got what he deserved. Knowing that that asshole named me Tina makes me so damn angry that I just want to be called by some other name, and I know the one I want. Call me Valerie."

"Valerie? Why?"

"It sounds like a strong name. Something I am. Not weak like Tina."

Flea nodded and simply said okay.

"Good. As for the plan," she drummed her fingers on her chin while her eyes bounced around, seeking nothing in the sky. "I saw your neighbor beating his dog the other day. But it wasn't the first time I seen he did it. What's his name?"

"Mr. Free."

"Yes, Mr. Free. Maybe we should teach him a lesson on how to properly treat animals. That poor little puppy doesn't deserve to be abused, and he ain't got the tools to defend himself. Say, Flea, you still got that gun?"

Flea hesitated to answer. He had many questions - questions that were likely to be met with conflict. Her heart had hardened. Every response she gave Flea today was cold and calloused. There was nothing he wanted more than to please her. So, he did just that. He simply nodded and left the questions in a lump in his throat.

CHAPTER FIVE

I t was later in the week and Mr. Free received a series of pounds at the door. He was startled awake by the metal clanging screen door. He scrunched up his leathery face and glanced over at the clock with his lifeless, gray eyes. The hour hand stretched to nine. "What the hell," he whispered to himself. His gray hair, matted in the back and missing up top, was tinged yellow on the tips from smoking in his home. The gin blossoms on his bulbous nose were especially vibrant this evening. A radiant purple. He scratched at his cauliflowered ears, and then dug into his whiskey-stained wife beater and tousled his sprawling chest hair.

The pounding at the door continued. His aging basset hound, gray in the muzzle and sweet to the core, howled toward the door. "Shut the hell up, Frank!" Mr. Free kicked his dog. The dog whimpered and scampered off towards his kennel with his overgrown claws clacking against the peel-n-stick vinyl tile beneath him. "Hold on a goddamn moment! Who the hell pounds on the door like this at this time of night anyway?" Mr. Free fit the bill of a nasty old man who held regard for no one - not even his loyal companion, Frank the wholesome basset hound. He wrenched the door handle and yanked it open where he found ~~Tina~~ Valerie, in tears. "What the hell do you want?"

"My dog, sir," Valerie sobbed. The night was pouring in and the sky was fading into a hue darker than navy blue. "He ran away."

His dead eyes looked past Valerie and scoured the streets and sidewalks, "I ain't seen no dog."

"He's a basset hound. A good ol' boy. He goes by Frank. Are you sure you haven't seen him?"

"Hey," he roared. His mouth shot open causing the skin to stretch some wrinkles clean, "What kind of sick trick are you trying to pull? I don't play that kind of shit!"

"I don't understand, sir. I'm looking for my dog. Don't you want to help me?"

"You better find some other dopey mother-fucker to fuck with and get your moo-cow ass the hell off my property before I put bullet in it."

"Sir! That is no way to talk to a little girl. I just want to find my doggie Frank." Behind the craggy old man Frank bellowed. "I think that's him!" Her finger jutted into the doorway as she said this, and Mr. Free smacked her hand away. He worked up his mouth to say something, but he was interrupted.

"Don't you dare touch her one more time," a voice threatened from behind Mr. Free.

"Oh yeah? And what the hell are you gonna do about it, you bug-eyed freak?" Mr. Free barked as he craned his neck around.

Flea peeled out of the shadows of a corner room with his pistol trained on Mr. Free. "Imma pull this trigger. That's what Imma do. So how bout you shut the hell up?"

"Who the hell do you think you are, kid? Come into *my* house and threaten me? You got a death wish kid! You think you can just bully me around with a gun. Bet you don't have any bullets for that thing anyway." With that, he charged toward Flea and closed the gap between the two in three full strides. Flea meant to pull the trigger but had forgotten he placed it on safe back at the creek. The tug came with no crash. A backhand sent the pistol flying towards the television, and a mighty right-hand clobbered Flea splaying him on the floor. For an old man, Mr. Free was tough and dogged. He wasn't going down without a fight. Flea tried to squirm backwards as Mr. Free was coming down on top of him, but he was unsuccessful. The old man pinned down Flea's stomach as he rained down punches. Flea crossed his arms in front of his face in defense. This wasn't the first time Flea had been pummeled, so he kept the presence of mind to seek a pattern. *Punch - Punch - Look - Punch - Punch - Look.* He wriggled around while Mr. Free continued to throw blows to his face and body. Next to the window was a baseball bat. Flea let down his guard after the next combination of punches came, and he stretched his hand out and grabbed the fat end of the bat. He came up short, and Mr. Free took advantage. *Punch - Punch - Crack -* Flea's head bounced off the threadbare carpet. Bright white stars blasted in his vision and he felt his lips and gums tingle. He faintly heard Valerie scream 'No!'. Like an obscure apparition, Valerie swooped in and tackled Mr. Free out of Flea's vision.

With one swift motion Flea swiped for the fat end of the bat and was able to palm it completely. He rolled to his knees. His sight settled, and the stars faded. He flipped the bat around and swung with a slugger's shot from hell to Mr. Free's temple. Flea's skin prickled as the ripple from the skull crack rattled its way down to the base of the bat. Shortly after, both Flea and Mr. Free blacked out. One from the blow, and the other from unmitigated rage.

Sluggish, Flea awoke on his haunches, over the man, with the bat planted to the floor for support. His chest heaved from heavy breaths while he wheezed and growled. There he witnessed what used to be Mr. Free. An eye dangled off to the side, while the other was buried under the rest of his caved in face. It pooled with blood on and around his head of matted gray hair. His gin-blossomed nose was somewhere in there. Flea knew that Mr. Free wasn't getting back up again, and the chills and worry that would normally shake him, shook him none. Valerie was behind him saying something, but nothing registered. She grew louder, and Frank's bellows from the back room grew.

"Flea, goddammit can't you hear me? Look at the mess you made!" He turned around trembling attempting to apologize, but she interrupted. "Don't be sorry! That was fantastic!" She hurried over and planted a kiss on his quivering lips. While Flea was collecting his nerves, Valerie ran off to let the dog out of its wired kennel.

Something unexpected happened. Frank raced past Flea and Valerie and rumbled over to Mr. Free. He paused to inspect his owner. The dog pivoted back and forth between where he was going to try and heal him first. As a part of his observation, Frank nudged his cold, wet nose into the dead man's wrist as if to take his pulse. He continued to prod the Mr. Free, but when Frank finally realized no response would come, he wedged his bulky head between Mr. Free's hand and belly and plopped his sorrowful body into the puddles of blood beneath him. With a deep sigh, and fluttering eyelids, he shot a stream of air over the corpse of his deceased owner.

An internal battle raged as Flea gaped down. His stomach lurched, and his skin was on fire. He wondered while he burned. How could a dog, who endured the brunt of an ill-tempered, uncontrollable man – nasty and scornful through every whip and punch and kick – stay faithful to such a degree that it would die happily in his arms?

Flea romanticized what should have happened. Frank leaping into his and Valerie's arms, lapping them with kisses and wag his tail so hard that it would whip them both on every swing, thanking them for rescuing him, and follow them to the ends of the earth. But he was wrong. He was profoundly wrong.

"Flea c'mon let's get out of here!" Valerie shouted. "Keep the bat, forget the dog. He was making an awful lot of noise while you were bashing that man's face in, and he don't seem too smart for wanting to stick around this dead guy."

Still, Flea was a wreck. He couldn't be moved. His good deed was not so. This dog needed someone to love, and the sole person in the world that he did love was ripped away from him. More-so bludgeoned to a pulp. Not even a sharp tug from Valerie could disrupt the constant churn of gears in his mind. His eyes grew wet as he stared intently at Frank, wishing he could bring back his awful and abusive owner, but there was no outcome that could produce such a result.

Valerie observed Flea's descent into depression, and knew she had to do something before they became the next great case of teenage murderers. She flipped on the sweet switch and said, "Flea, look, I can tell you're feeling bad for the dog, and I do too, but remember how awful this man was to him." She placed herself in his view. "This doesn't change how rotten of a man Mr. Free was. Just think about all the awful things your mother has done to you. You wouldn't be a lost, little puppy dog if she was gone, would you?"

Flea shook his head and said, "No, I can't stand that woman."

"I know, honey," she acknowledged. "That just means this dog isn't smart enough to know how good he could have it instead. Once the cops come, and they'll be here soon, which is why we *must* get out of here, they'll be sure to take Frank and they'll find him a good home. A much better one, where a whole family can love him and treat him

155

decently. Do you believe me? Please tell me you do." He nodded and remained silent. Some of her familiar sweetness returned, which Flea had been missing since Tina slipped into this Valerie character. The faint feeling comforted Flea, but only for a moment. From a distance the sounds of sirens were filling the room. "C'mon Flea, we have to go," Valerie urged Flea along and along he went.

They went their separate ways for the evening – Valerie went home, and Flea returned to the creek to spend another blink-less night among the dirt and trees. He crouched over the moonlit waters and reached in, swishing his hands around. He rapidly dipped his hands in and raised them creating a fluid cyclical motion. Water droplets sparkled like crystals in a mine. The taste of iron flowed to his lips as the water rinsed the globs of blood from his forehead. With all the chaos storming in his mind, he lost sight of the bat. Before cleansing himself, he carelessly propped the bat up against a tree. It slipped off the trunk and tumbled down the bank and splashed into the creek. Merrily down the stream it went, and Flea worried none. Only the coolness of the splash beating against his face could soothe his battered heart.

Sagging winds swept through him and sent a chill up his spine. An unsettling notion rocked him. Everything that had happened made him think a terrifying thought. How long would they be able to kill people, bad people, but people nonetheless, without being caught? Flea wasn't a smart kid, but he knew well enough that killing any single person, regardless of their cruel nature, was against the law, and a very serious law at that.

He woke up bleary-eyed and terrified. Throughout the night he woke up to haunting hour disturbances. Rustling leaves, slashing waters, and howling winds kept his nerves keyed up and his alert meter bending on hypervigilant. Still numb from sleeplessness and agitation, he hopped on his bike and hatched a plan as he wore the rubber from his bike tires on the way to Valerie.

Huffing and puffing, Flea ghost rode the bike into a nearby gnarled oak tree as he sprinted to the front of Valerie's home. He pounded and pounded on the warped aluminum door as his chest heaved with rapid sucking breaths. "Valerie..." he said with half of his breath, the other half spluttered out like air from a gashed tire. Footsteps rumbled from beyond the door.

"Hello?" Valerie's mother answered.

"Hi Mrs. Tramper," Flea announced, gaining some wind in his lungs, "is Val... I mean is... is Tina home?"

"Why sure she is," she responded. "C'mon in Flea. What's the matter?"

"Oh nothin'. I was thinking about her and just wanted to check on her with all that's going on lately."

"What a thoughtful thing to do Flea. She's very lucky to have a friend like you. I'll go get her."

She let him in through the door and proceeded to call on Tina. No response.

"Hold on a moment, Flea. I kept her home from school since she probably isn't ready to deal with school and everything. Let me see if she's in her room."

She walked down the hall and faded out of view. He bent forward and placed his hands on his knees where his breath finally caught up with him. Flea looked around the home and caught an eerie vibe. It hung low like a tired, drooping clothesline. He felt his stomach form into a square knot, but this time it hadn't cinched tight. Sweat bunched up on his forehead and slow-dripped its way down and around every pimple and pock mark in his skin.

157

The recliner Mr. Tramper laid dead in had been removed, but Flea couldn't be teased that it didn't happen as the floor was still stained from the blood - a dark brown now ruined the carpet from Mrs. Tramper's scrubbing brush. He looked away for fear of remembering, but his mind was already at work painting on a mental canvass, filling the space with vivid detail. After several hard head shakes and forceful blinks, he looked back to the spot where the deed was done. For a moment he saw him sitting in the chair again, stewing in a bloody mess. That moment lingered as the sound of buzzing flies filled his ears. They darted around the dead body and drifted closer and closer – *Buzz*- They bounced off the windows and light fixtures. The buzzing grew louder - *Buzz* – Flea felt them breathing on him as they now zipped around his head - *BUZZZZZZZZ*. His arms flailed attempting to fend off the persistent flies, but persistent they were, and they filled the air. Repeatedly, he slapped at his neck - brushed at his cheeks – scratched his hair – swatted at air. He swatted at nothing. They weren't actually there, but his mind would not let him believe it. The flies would just be there, always darting around him and flying too close for comfort, but never landing. They never landed.

Soon, that wouldn't matter. The reanimation of Mr. Tramper's corpse began. Once lifeless and immobile, his limbs jerked and kicked and were being drawn up like strings from a marionette with spasmodic hands. Flea's jaw unhinged in disbelief, gaping at what could not possibly be. Mr. Tramper's clothes peeled from the recliner; the noise resembling Velcro slowly being ripped apart. The sound echoed in Flea's ears and possessed his nerves. He grimaced in horror as the body of Mr. Tramper floated to his feet. The corpse peered out of the window, gazing into the midmorning sun. Flea let out an audible gasp. The decaying man sharply turned his bullet-holed face towards the panic-stricken boy. Flesh hung like a tired dog tongue from his cheeks, his gnashing teeth exposed from the opening in his face. Those same dead, black eyes narrowed as he sized-up Flea. The zombie laughed, the sound like a growl chopping through a ceiling fan. "Looks like your life is ruined now isn't it, Flea?" his voice gurgled in a deep, sunless tone. "Shoulda listened to me when you had the chance, Flea. Now yer just another sad, sad case. Gon' be locked up for the rest of yer pathetic life now, Flea. It is Flea, isn't it?" The corpse's grave, hollow laugh struck Flea in the center of his chest. It leapt as Mr. Tramper hobbled his way over to Flea, ramping up speed as he stumbled closer. A fresh breath of air was knocked clean out of Flea's chest as he shuddered in terror. The dead man drew up his arms to wrap Flea up. Instead, the young boy rolled his eyes into the back of his head and sank with gravity.

Mrs. Tramper shook Flea a few times until he regained consciousness. He was on the floor now. His arms shot out and then back in to grab his chest, gasping for air. Cool sweat draped him like a spring rain. He swallowed hard and looked over at Mrs. Tramper. She offered him a hand up. As she did so, she asked concernedly, "Flea, my goodness! Are you ok?"

"Yeah, I'm okay." He wasn't.

She knew, but continued anyway, "I was just in Tina's bedroom and she wrote me a note saying she'd run away and changed her name to..."

"Valerie..." Flea interjected. In a fit of exasperation and vulnerability Flea blurted, "Listen, it was me that did it, not Brick. I did it. It was me!"

"I'm sorry honey, what do you mean? And her name, how did you know she changed it?"

"She told me after I killed yer... yer husband. I'm terribly sorry Mrs. Tramper, but I hafta go find her. I think I know where she ran off-ta."

Mrs. Tramper turned red and shouted, but by the time the words worked their way out of her mouth Flea had already bolted through the creaky aluminum door and towards the knobby oak tree where his trusty steed awaited. He set course for the place where he and Valerie first, and ever, felt alone.

With his frame now dented like discount canned goods and his tires the shape of eggs, the trek was now more labored and arduous. The wheels screamed under the demand of Flea's pedaling, stretching what little life the bike had left. It came to the point of the route where Flea had to bump over the curb, but this time he was too exhausted to pull up the front of the bike beforehand. He slammed into the curb and was sent careening over the handlebars. He flipped and landed flat on his back, stealing whatever wind was left in his sails. Flea, and the bike, was smoked.

Before he could think about getting up, his face flopped grass-ward and observed a crow pecking at the eyes of a decaying squirrel. The black bird's feathers shimmered in the sunny beams, casting brilliant shades of iridescent greens and purples on her back and wing tips. She drove her beak down and then back up, down and up, her tiny neck twitching and repeating, rending the orb from its socket. Muscles held fast to the eye, clutched as if it even mattered anymore. Like a rubber band snapped, the muscle gave way on the other end, flinging globs of blood on both the bird and the grass. Deep in the crow's maw was a throaty cackling caw. Her razor beak acted as chopsticks hoisting the orb proudly with the meaty strand dangling like a twisting limp noodle. It cackled again, so sinister – almost as if it were laughing.

Flea laid there transfixed. Could this have been his imagination playing tricks on him again? Something told him this was real, and it was happening, but another piece of him denied it.

The crow already tossed the eye aside and dug back into the cavity, scrambling the tiny brain inside.

How was this happening while Flea was laying there watching? Wasn't the crow perturbed by his presence? Clearly not. It continued to draw up grey matter, opened her beak, and slipped it down her gullet.

Flea had his fill. His breath had been restored, but his stomach squirmed with the vulgarity of the raven carnage. And so, he shot to his feet. The crow slid down another morsel, cawed again, seemingly directly at Flea, and set to the sky with her fabulous black and green and purple wings flapping unhurriedly and carefree. Flea shook off the creepshow with a series of shrugs, and head jerks. He and his flappy shoes made their way back into the forest where Valerie and he had spent so much time before his brothers brought their hands of irreparable destruction.

The shack was still in shambles, but Valerie was there, perched quizzically on the ground with her legs gathered in her arms, and her face screwed up in consternation. It was clear something was amiss, that much Flea discerned, but what bothered him were the scissors next to her and her locks of golden hair scattered across the dirt. She was unbound. She had been before when her anger consumed her, but she was now altogether despondent and floating in uncertainty.

"Valerie," Flea squeaked, "are you okay?"

She shivered out of deep contemplation and glared up at Flea. A blizzard was brewing in her eyes and he felt cold just by the stare. Without a word, she returned her gaze to the destructed shack.

"I... I had to tell your mom about," a lump formed in his throat, but he swallowed it down and continued, "ya know, yer dad and what happened."

Again, she was unresponsive. She offered nothing. Her pink arms were crawling with goosebumps. The world could have been on fire all around her and she would have sat there unmoved waiting for the flames to take her home. In a single fluid motion, she sighed deeply and sunk her shoulders a little further. Still, her lips were thin lines and closed for business.

"Are... are ya mad?" Flea prodded, hoping to get something out of her.

She shook her head slowly, never removing her eyes from the planks of wood scattered across the dirt floor.

Flea was put off. He wasn't sure what steps he would need to take next to get to Valerie. All he wanted was her help. He had a thought germinating in his mind, but it wasn't fleshed out quite yet. There was a plausible ending to curt all the impending doom suspended above their heads. He needed confirmation. He needed Valerie to say something. Anything. So, instead of telling her what he wanted to do, he asked, "What do we do now?"

She buried her head and growled, "Can't you figure anything out on your own? Do I have to do everything for you?"

"Well, no... I mean I had an idea and..."

"Would you look at that," Valerie snapped and popped her head out from between her legs. "Flea has an idea everybody, let's listen in on this. This should be good."

"You don't hafta be so rude," Flea replied in a small voice. He was hurt but didn't want to shrink away into helplessness like he normally did. The sun burned his skin as he stood as tall as his bones would allow. This time Valerie would hear him and accept him. This time was going to be different. And so, with his feet planted in the earth below and his chest bulged out he said, "I think things too, Valerie. And they might not be as good as yours – or as big as yours, but they matter. It ain't fair that you git angry at me whenever I got a question. You been steerin' this whole thing start-to-finish, so who am I to stick my foot out and stop you?" His chest hissed and popped as he exhausted what little breath he had inside. "Now, I know yer tired, but so am I. I want me to matter to you, and I think I do. Don't I, Valerie? And the things I think, they matter too, right?"

Her heart was a smoldering fire pit, yet the embers inside were alive being stoked by the wind of Flea's words. She flashed back to when she was Tina and thought of the kind things she would say to him when he needed her most. Those memories trembled underneath her skin and sent her into chills. Valerie's heart had become guarded, preventing encroachment from the hate out in the world, keeping them at bay with the bulwark – so much so, she forgot who she had been. A kind spirit who wanted nothing but to guide the weak into deliverance. "I'm sorry Flea, I'm just so tired. Being this mad for this long does something to a person. It hurts, and it aches. Something doesn't feel quite right. I'm afraid that I can't do it anymore. You know, kill bad people. But this world, this trailer park alone, is full of them and I hate them. They're awful. And I just don't think I wanna live in this world anymore." Valerie shriveled up and locked her eyes to the ground between her knobby knees. She didn't cry, but her shuddered breath hinted to the tears that were to come. And they came. A flash flood gushed from her eyes and she tried desperately to catch the tears that fell, but they were too many, and streamed down different curves of her round cheeks, and the others bounced just beyond her fingertips.

Flea swooped down on Valerie, his wiry arm sliding over her shoulder blades, while the other collected tears from the source. He wiped her eyes with a crooked thumb and huddled closer to speak to her as if they needed privacy from the earth around them. He whispered softly in her ear, "What if we didn't have to?"

"What do you mean?" she asked in returned as tears were pumping slower and slower now; easing up like an automated brake system, then stopping completely. As she did this, she twisted towards him yet reeling away from him, so she could see all of his face. Every pock and divot became sharp in her sight. She painted his face with her eyes as she waited for an answer.

"Well," Flea started, "I feel the same way. I'm tired of fighting everyone all the time. We don't get respect from no-one, no matter how hard we try. Even if we do try, they'd look at us like trash no matter what anyway. 'Specially once they find out what we done they'd want nuthin' to do with us. It won't get no better. We can choose our own destiny. Go the way we want to go, not how *they* want us to go." He felt that same power he felt when he had told off those terrible peers of theirs. It coursed in his veins. It gave him strength. "Let's do it Valerie."

A blanket of relief warmed her. She had orchestrated every movement since they decided to do the dirty work of ridding the enormity of the world. Now, she could breathe. Nice and easily. Flea saw the warmth glow into her skin again. He kept his eyes on her studying her knowing that soon she would agree to his proposal. And she did, "Yes... let's do it. But, let's make it count."

CHAPTER SIX

L ater that evening the stars bled against the night sky. The heat of the day had relented to a warm buzz with shifting winds cutting the temperature to a bearable degree. In his muscle shirt and jeans torn at the knees, Flea found himself breathing on the metal grated storm door. This was the time. Right here. Right now. The final act. Tension formed in his shoulders and neck building golf-ball sized stress-knots throughout his scrawny little body, but the usual square knots that upset his stomach never made an appearance.

Flea burst through that door. His fat mother, startled, bounced in the chair. She had been laying boneless in her bottoming-out chair, but the jolt sent her cascading backwards. The cheap lumber in the chair splintered under the immense pressure; the nails that had been glued in peeled away with the ease of a ripe banana; boards within shot out tearing cloth with wood claws. With a thunderous clap, the back of her head struck the linoleum floor, but not before she caught her neck on the case of bargain soda hidden behind the chair. An audible crack rumbled to Flea's flappy shoes. The soda popped; fizz casted corn syrup graffiti on the walls and floor.

His mom howled in pain, screaming "Gaht dammit!" Her arms laid flat on the ground and her legs sprawled out resting somewhat on the remnants of the recliner. A can of soda rolled out of the cardboard sleeve and wheeled over to her side, gushing the contents on her face and neck. "What the fuck! *AAAAGGGGHHHHH!* My gaht damn neck! Jee-zus Christ! Sunnuva-bitch!"

"There you go again ma," Flea spoke flatly. "Talkin' bad about yer-self."

"Flea? Is that you?" She shouted in pain. For the life of her, she couldn't strain her neck to twist her head in any direction. It was pinned between the folded, pillowy neck rest of the chair, but she feared that even if there hadn't been the obstruction of recliner rubble, she wouldn't have been able to look around anyway.

"The one and only. Havin' problems, Ma?"

"Flea don't you give me any sass you little asshole. Get over here!"

"Gladly." Flea strode over with swagger. He held a five-gallon gas jug in one hand, that sloshed with each step he took, and in the other a long-neck funnel.

"What's that you got there with you?" She prodded.

"Don't you mind that noise; you'll find that out soon enough."

A second set of footsteps echoed Flea as he drew nearer and nearer to his Mother. She strained her neck more to look at what was happening, but again she was stuck. In fact, she couldn't move anything below her neck. She called on her brain to move something. Anything. Her lips were numb and trembling. No matter what she told her mind to move it felt as if the rest of her body was unplugged at every outlet. "FLEA," she cried fearfully, "WHAT THE HELL IS HAPPENING?

I can't feel nothing! And who is that with you? I hear someone else. Who is that?!"

"It don't matter who it is Ma."

"It's okay, Flea," Valerie interjected. As she spoke to his mother, she dragged a metal-head sledgehammer behind her. It produced a dull scratch across the floor. "We haven't been properly introduced. My name is Valerie, and I'm your son's girlfriend."

"Girlfriend?" Flea's mother scoffed. "What kind of girl would wanna date Flea?"

"I think any decent person would Miss," Valerie said surprisingly respectful, as if she cared about a great first impression, but to a person who didn't deserve it. "No one really has given him the time of day, and I happen to think he is a kind soul that gives and gives and gives but doesn't get a whole lot in return. All that giving and not enough getting can really damage a person's soul, don't-cha-think?"

"What the hell do you know?"

Unfazed, Valerie continued, "I guess not a whole lot. Ya know what, though? Flea's told me a lot 'bout you. You're not a very nice person – and that we do *know* – that is something we do know that *we* do not like." Both Flea and Valerie appeared above the paralyzed woman and peered down. "And lately, that has been something both Flea and I, have been addressing with certain folks. We been taking matters into our own hands about people who aren't very nice. And you, ma'am, happen to fit the bill."

"Wait," Flea's mother paused her, "You're that little Tramper girl, ain't you?"

"The same. Got a new haircut, like it?" Uneven layers of blonde hair were bounced by her free hand. "Anyway – what was I sayin'? Oh yeah, certain folks and bills. My dad wasn't very nice. You probably wouldn't know that, but you probably wouldn't care. Hell, you'd probably've gotten along well with him. So, Flea and I had to get rid of him."

"You rotten little shit! You two framed my poor, sweet Brick! And now he's gone forever. I'm going to wring your neck!"

"I'm sorry Ma'am, but you aren't going to do shit," Valerie replied with a lilt, staring below at the gelatinous mass. "Your son was an asshole. He treated your son like a waste basket. I'd tell you what he used to do to Flea when he was around, but I'd be wasting my breath. You probably'd get a kick out of it with your *cold* black heart. And so, we threw him into a bigger wastebasket. The biggest one we could find. Prison. I find it mighty fitting. He'll never feel freedom again, and he can have you to thank, since your top-notch parenting is what really got him there in the first place."

"Shut up, you stupid little girl!" Flea's mother bellowed. Every muscle in her body betrayed her, laying stiffly as the fat pooled around her bones filing into empty spaces between the broken parts of the chair. Wood dug into her thin skin, cutting her without her knowledge. Blood bubbled all around her. All she could feel was the needling sting in her neck and the pulsing fear in her heart.

"Ya see this?" Valerie dangled the ten-pound sledgehammer with both hands and let it sway precariously above her head. "We were going to use this to bust you down, but it looks like you and your chair had a falling out of sorts. Took care of the heavy lifting for us." Valerie snickered at her back-to-back jabs.

"You ain't got no gaht damn manners, you snakey little bitch. Who the hell do you think you are? I won't be havin' any more of this sh..."

What she was planning to say next, we'll never know. Flea shoved the long-neck funnel into his mother's mouth and knelt on her chest to get stable. He clamped the hose between both knees and drove it further into her throat which produced a gag fit to send her into vomiting. She tried to speak, but the rubber hose threatened to break through her esophageal lining. All she could muster was *Nnnnnggg-nng-nnnnnnggggg-uuurrrgggll-ggguuulllrrr.*

"Alright ma, you done enough talkin'. It's my turn." This was the time for Flea to slough off the skin of who he had been, and who he was now going to be. He took a deep breath through his nose. No more would he be the family punching bag. A change was going to come. He let out the breath and started. "You were a terrible mother. I say *were* cuz Valerie and I are gonna fix that. All I wanted was to be loved and accepted, but you treated me like I was nothin'. No, not nothin', cuz then at least I'da been free from your tire-a-nee. You treated me like a soccer ball. You kicked me around and let me bounce off feet and hands and walls and streets and tables and sidewalks until I wasn't fun no more. And you let mah brothers do the same." Tears welled as he choked on the swelling pain in his throat from battling the sadness. The fight was well fought, but it was all for naught. The tears came furiously from his eyes anyway. With that came sucking breaths, the kind that do what they might to stymie the overwhelming congestion in his heart. "They punished me, Ma. And you sat there. Sat there on yer big fat ass while I bled, Ma. From ass to elbows I bled, and I ain't ever known why. What did I do to deserve this, Ma?

"Yer to blame for mah pain," He spat the words out, the saliva marking his mother. His face still raining. "My years on this world have been a damn sitcom to you and mah brothers, 'cept there ain't no laughing track. Just a cruel hard memory that sleeps in mah head every night. I tossed, and I turned but I could have rolled down a hill before I felt the calm most folks feel at night. But that changed when I met Tin... I mean Valerie." The misnomer took him aback, shaking his head violently to milk the sudden venom in his veins. "She loves me the way

I am, and now I'm gonna stop you from being mean to me ever again. Wish it coulda been different, but it is what it is." A final twinkling tear grouped at the corner of Flea's eye as he truly wished it could have been different. Being crusty and cruel corroded his soul, but he felt that there were no other options for him and Valerie. This is how it had to be.

He swiped at his weepy eye with his wrist, wiping the sole bubbling tear that threatened to fall. "I think that's a-nuff words, now." Once he delivered the eulogy, pre-humous, Flea popped the cap off the nozzle and lifted the cumbersome gas can with both hands. It wobbled and threatened to jump from his grasp as his scrawny arms drew it up. The gasoline sloshed up the sides and nearly spat out the top. He steadied the can by placing his left hand on the bottom for a surer base.

"Down the hatch," said Flea while he poured. The funnel gulped and gurgled as Flea's mother's lungs received the fuel. The fumes stripped his hands of moisture. They grew ashy and itchy. The tiny hairs in his nose curled. More tears involuntarily piped to the surface, hotter than the kick-back of the tear-searing gasoline.

His mother's chest rose, but not from breath. The gas had filled where it could and bloated in the belly, seeming to find enough skin to stretch it to maximum capacity. The gasoline galloped from the can and strode in with crashing waves. She gargled and spat what she could, but her lips were gaped by the hose, so her efforts were fruitless. Her tongue flailed under the black hose. If she could have moved her body, she would have thrashed and kicked and made this trailer home tremble beneath her and brought it down to the cement blocks they stood on. Instead she sat there in fat mess ingesting two-and-a-half gallons of gas.

Flea removed the hose after a while. Fuel dribbled out of the sides of her motionless mouth. First it pooled at her lips, zapping any dignity of wetness from them. Then the fuel sank back into her body finding real estate in the third of her many chins. Her eyes bulged, shoving the eyelids to their respective positions. They were cold and gray, with a look of fear frozen on her kinked eyebrows. The look chilled both Flea and Valerie.

With heavy arms, Flea dropped the half-drained gas can. This time no black out came. This was a self-assurance that what they had planned had to be done.

Flea plunged deep into his pockets and groped around for the box of matches he stashed. He drew them up like a yo-yo. "Are you ready, Valerie?" he asked eagerly.

Her lips said yes, but her eyes said no.

He placed the matches on the kitchen counter and wrapped his hands around the handle of the gas can. With white knuckles and the last of his energy, Flea splashed the floor around his mother and trailed it from there. He walked backwards, the muscles in his quads burning as he steered around the narrow passageway of the kitchen into the skinny hallway. At the end of the hall was the room where the twins and Stone sleep. They weren't home. Flea thought back to that day he was beaten in the street for reading that comic book. When it had been shredded and thrown in his face, while they spat on him and called him those crude names. His teeth gnashed as he whipped liquid ropes of gas on their beds and all their favorite things including footballs, hockey sticks, and bats festooned with sharp objects; ones that had gouged him more than a few times over the years.

He trampled over to the bathroom and splashed fuel in the corners, toilet, and bathtub.

From there he went to the room where he thought he could be safe all those years. That little corner in life where he could curl up into a tiny ball, in the darkest corner of the world, and let the square knots slip and ease him into comfort. He flicked the gas can, now reduced to a three-finger line along the bottom, into that creature comfort. He wanted it to burn, but not with the malice he held for the rest of the house.

Then he saw it. Brick's *nut-rag* sitting on his nightstand. Flea's eyes grew large and hateful. That rag had been the source of so much pain. Whenever he felt the warm blanket of his fully darkened room, in Brick would come, *nut-rag* and all, and smash it into Flea's face, wrenching his wrists and scrubbing as if he were deep cleaning and exfoliating the skin. Flea raged as he hefted the gas can high above his head. He doused the rag, fuel plopping onto the nightstand spilling down its sides. The pungent sting of fuel ripened within his nostrils. An odd sense of satisfaction flashed over him as the crusted *nut-rag* had flattened from gas. Soaked and defeated.

The fever ceased, and he pored over Brick's bed. He pictured Brick laying there, wishing he could empty shotgun shells into him until the body was marred to the point beyond recognition. That wouldn't do, since he was off laying in some steel slab in the juvenile detention center waiting to be arraigned for a crime he never committed. Sure, that should please him, but Flea wanted Brick to writhe in his hands. He wanted to feel Brick fight for his life, thrash with his arms and legs, plead to be released, but to be deprived of that request. To feel the life slowly drain out of Brick's body and absorb it through the transference of contact. That simply couldn't happen, so Flea improvised. He stuffed what pillows laid on the bed under the covers to make it seem like Brick was in bed, unsuspecting of what was to come next. Flea shook out the rest of the fuel like he was rebuking a demon from it. Even when the last drop had fallen, Flea convulsed with that can flopping in his hands until madness stole his breath and the sadness settled. He wailed and casted the can aside, bouncing off the bedroom window.

Valerie detected the commotion and ran over to the source. There, she spotted Flea crumbled in a pile, sucking breath as he bawled.

He howled as if he was hurt, but the pain wasn't on the surface. Valerie could see that. Somewhere beneath the skin his heart bled slow and his intestines twisted, forming that same square knot he knew too well. She placed her hand on his shoulder. He received it warmly as the cool touch soothed him and stifled the tears to a shuddering close. "C'mon Flea," Valerie whispered, "we have to do this now." He nodded and got to his feet.

They stood in the kitchen, Flea with matches in hand. "Before we torch this place to the ground," Valerie started while twisting the sledgehammer handle, the head spinning on the linoleum. "I just want to say a few things. These past few months have been the best of my life. Before I met you, I was slipping into a bottomless depression. I didn't want to hurt anymore. I wanted to die. But then you came along. Sure, we still faced terrible times and went through some things that no single person should ever have to experience, but you were there to help me through. So... thank you, for saving me." Her arms wrapped around Fleas waist and she planted a kiss on his lips so soft and sweet. "I love you, Flea. And I always will. No matter where we go from here. My only hope is that I will see you again."

They continued to embrace as tears poured from Flea's face into the remaining curls of Valerie's summer sun hair. "I love you too, Val." In sobbing breaths, Flea pushed her away, but kept her close enough to peer into her two blue pools, "We will see each other again. I promise you." She nodded as she wiped away the water from her eyes.

It happened so fast. Once Flea tossed the struck match flames roared through the hallway, reaching their fiery arms to the back-half of the trailer. The fuel-soaked bathroom and bedrooms were eaten by flames. Stone and the Twins room. Gone. The bathroom. Gone. Both were engulfed in the matter of seconds.

The mock *Brick-in-bed* was suffocated in smoke. Flames came quickly after, eating at the corners then swallowing the bed whole. The pillows writhed under the covers. Then, it spread to the nightstand. The *nut-rag* crumpled into a charred chunk of fabric. Like piecemeal, the closet was next, consumed by orange heat. The walls peeled away to the ceiling, running from the tongues of flame failing in their attempt as they caught fire anyway.

Flames chewed through the walls, the shifting winds outside created an inward gust, blowing the orange glow about them, but not directly touching them. The backdraft was strong enough to make them tremble where they stood, but they remained firmly planted on their feet. Fire found its way around the young lovers, cutting a path between them, raised like tiny garden gates, finding another source of energy in Flea's dead mother. His mother blazed in a brilliant fireball. Sweat burst from every pore as the temperature climbed. Soon enough they would be gone, but that didn't matter to them anymore. This is what they wanted. This was it. There was no turning back.

They gazed lovingly into each other's eyes as blazing trails separated them. The back-half of the trailer became a blistering orange-red wall. They watched as the ceiling gave way, barricading the front door. This torrid little trailer home recreated their own inferno, and all they could do was smile as they peered deeply into each other.

Flea wanted to shout *I love you* before the moment passed, but a sudden swell erupted from his mother. The fuel inside of her had caught up with the rest of the home and thrust out smacking the unsuspecting Flea and sent him reeling into a wall. He ricocheted and dove, belly down, into the place where he was once standing.

He rolled to his back. An ember from the ceiling drifted and landed squarely on his eyeball. He wanted to shriek, but he had no breath. He wanted to flail, but he had no energy. All he could do was listen to it sizzle as he batted his eyelashes attempting to brush it away but being nothing but unsuccessful. He remembered the crow that had mercilessly separated the squirrel's eye from its socket. Something in the pain of his smoldering eye told him that this must be what it feels like. The world in that eye ceased to exist.

Inhalation exhaustion dug at Flea's grave, but death was a warm invitation now. His neck became weak, and his head heavy. His head rocked back to where Valerie was standing, but she wasn't there. She was there, but not where she had been. With his final view of his world ablaze, and his remaining good eye, he observed Valerie with her back turned. Grunting, she drew up the sledgehammer and came down with mighty force, hacking through the wreckage before the door. She cleared the path and as she walked out, she glanced back to look at Flea and blew him a kiss mouthing the words, '*I'm sorry.*'

NODS

efore I go thanking people, I want to thank a place.
Most famous authors benefit coming from popular
locations with notable landmarks and have the luxury
of relying on the commonality of people being familiar with the
destination. Minnesota is not generally on this list, but I couldn't
tell you why it isn't. You can find beauty of every variety. The
Twin Cities has everything a big city needs – hipster cafes,
independent boutiques, major sports teams (SKOLLL), THE
MALL OF AMERICA, and art (tons of it – everywhere [support
it!]). From there, you can drive thirty minutes in almost any
direction and catch a whiff of pastoral landscapes – horses
running the fields, ponds large enough to be considered lakes in
most states, forests flush with treetops touched by autumn rust –

at the same time – crowded with indeterminate folklores which cause children, and adults alike, to keep away from the wood-line when the sun goes down. Some days I still take my trash out at night and run right back in – ya know – just in case something, or someone, is somewhere out there between my neighbor's pine trees. Minnesota has everything you need in life. Stop by and visit.

Three years ago, I wrote the roughest version of my first short story. I had just sworn off writing anymore Fantasy Football articles. I was too encumbered by school, work, and providing for the fam. My closest friend reached out to me – if he wasn't so "Ron Swanson" about keeping off the grid, I would share his name and thank him publicly, but for the sake of naming the guy we'll dub him Rusty Shackleford. He asked me if I ever thought about writing fiction, and I had a lapse in memory. At first, I told him, "not really", but that wasn't true. I had written some of the worst stories when I was a teenager, under the influences of – ermmm – let's call it peer pressure. Yeah. I like that.

Anyway, Rusty pitched a story to me about a deaf man who gets a cochlear implant and instead of reveling in the spoils of natural sounds and beauty, he hears a voice which is not there. He lobbed this lump of clay that would become *It's Beautiful Isn't It* and left it up to me to shape it how I saw fit. Being that R.S. is such a close friend of mine, he knew that I might have an inkling about how the scenario might play out (being a child of a deaf adult somehow gives me an edge?). The only thing he wanted in return was to ride my coattails when I shoot off into superstardom, but he didn't want to seem like too much of a schlub, so I'm supposed to let him be my agent or something. At any rate, thank you Mr. Shackleford for a hair-brained idea that just might work *I think these people like it.*

Next, I thank my cousin, Justin. He is the biggest horror fan I know, and I know a lot of them. His feedback has been invaluable in each one of these stories, and if you know him you might even feel some of his presence in them. Hell, some have even been written for him. So, thank you Primo for your faithfulness in your helpfulness.

Clearly, my parents must be thanked. They bore me into this world. They taught me stuff. They kept me alive (which is no feat to scoff at – I was a rambunctious little guy trying to impress everybody in every physically possible way). Dad, thank you for always being curious and hungry to learn. In turn, that made me a curious person who hungered to learn – funny how that works out, huh? And Mom, God I miss you. As a tiny little tyke, I watched with wonder how natural the creative juices coursed your veins. You twisted wire into trees, topped the branches with bits of amethyst, and planted them on broad stones; you made felt top-hats out of one-gallon ice cream buckets and cardboard; and you always were the star of the show when it came time to 'dressing for the occasion'. I long for the day we see each other again, but until then save me a seat next to you, wherever you are.

Lastly, there would be no stories without the next person. I mean, there would be stories, but they wouldn't be worth their weight in scratch paper. Her magnificent brain has brought texture to some of my most important work. Without her, a couple of these stories wouldn't even exist. This woman is my soul. She is my muse. She is my wife. Thank you love, you're worth the whole damn bunch put together.

Also, my daughter. You inspire me every day with your injections of clever phrases and witty banter. May you never read a word of this book until... I don't know... hopefully never – but if you do just know that Daddy is a happy person. He just likes to write dark stuff.

A great deal of people took their time reading these stories one by one (looking at you Eli, Steve, Warren, and Jesse). They watched me sculpt these damn things into the passable stories they are now. There are a lot of you, and I'm sorry I did not shout you out precisely but know in your hearts that each bit of feedback you supplied was taken into consideration and/or implemented. So, for that I'm eternally grateful.

AUTHOR NOTES

This section is for the readers who like to delve into the minds of writers. To crack the skull and peer through the oozy sheen of gray matter to see what prompted these stories.

Truth be told, I love talking about them in such intimate fashion. These are my babies that have spent several years germinating in the petri dish of my mind so I could blather about them until my eyes are dry and scratchy, or in this case type until carpal tunnel ravages my wrists (I have poor typing form and I don't care who knows it).

"Get on with it!" Yeah, I hear you. Without further ado, here is the inside scoop on each story.

WE ARE ACID 77

I don't mention this a whole lot on social media platforms or conversations with random people in real life, but I am in the military and will likely continue to be as long as the checks clear. My service isn't a well-kept secret, but it is something that I do not broadcast.

Every year, the *powers that be* whisk me away for a couple of weeks to wherever they please to do whatever the hell they deem necessary. This is what they call Annual Training (AT). Several years ago, this story was born from that year of AT. Outside of the supernatural occurrences, and the characters in We are Acid 77 this is a true story. Another soldier and I were called to pull a vague duty called guard training. Once guard training was revealed as performing guard duty at an observation point, for a twelve-hour swing, we were sent to sit out on a field that had not been occupied by humans for quite some time. Several hours passed and, while in a zombified state, I peered out into the wood line because my paranoid mind was dutifully at work, when a flash of something brown streaked by in my periphery. Given the heat and humidity it was likely one out of a million bugs whooshing by, but my mind doesn't naturally shove that notion aside. There I was, out in the field crafting this story at that very moment, typing furiously into my phone paragraph after paragraph.

The title came to me after being given a call sign for a convoy route later that same AT. We were told that the call sign would be Acid Seven-Seven. To this day, it's the oddest call sign I've been given but I'm thankful.

LIFE IS BUT A DREAM

As I mentioned in my nods, my wife loves to share her story ideas with me and expects me to write them as if my pen (keyboard) is the play and the page is the stage in her mind. My daughter was singing *Row Your Boat* while my wife was brushing her hair. Then, she got this eerie vision of a guy out in his boat where he hears this being sung in a dense fog. She pitched it to me and I went to work!

Gus exists because he reminds me of my neighbor who is the best neighbor anyone can ask for. He owns every tool a person would ever need, he mows a little over the line on our shared lawn, and he drops off fudge on our doorstep every Christmas (and let me tell you the fudge is exquisite!). Like Gus, he is a retired widower with not much to do but keep himself busy with his yard and wood-working projects. I can hear you say, "Why are you killing your neighbors, C. J.?!" and I'll just say – first, mind your business – and second, I don't see Gus's end as a hate-filled murder, but more of a mercy ending to bring two long lost loves back together again. And if my neighbor ever reads this, I hope he feels that same way.

THE BONE CLOWN

This special guy came to me in a dream. Or a nightmare. Whichever helps you sleep at night. Whatever you want to call it, he was a part of what was a marathon of horror baddies sprinting from one spicy situation to the next. I struggle to recall the entire cast, except for two of them. One being the possessed co-worker who snuck into my bed (I was a perfect gentleman), and The Bone Clown. Throughout the hellish dreamscape, nothing crossed me up quite like the latter. Much like the other figments of my imagination, he burned into my thoughts. He coursed my veins as if he were poison and made it impossible for me to get on with my daily routine without some sort of interruption. The only way I was going to be able to get him out was to purge him through a story.

According to others who have enjoyed this story, he deserves a sequel, and dammit I just might do it. When? Not a clue, but it would be with another character from one of the stories in this collection.

HELL'S HALF ACRE

This is a real place out by where I grew up. Now, Mr. Gunnersen, was a flair for the dramatics, but the legend of Hell's Half Acre was if any trespasser were caught on said property, they were *ahem* dispatched *ahem* and stuffed into a culvert.

What I tried to capture on this story was an experience that I personally had, but certainly not to the degree or severity of what occurred in the tale of the two in Hell's Half Acre. Back in high school, I spent the night over at a friend's house and with us stayed another close friend of mine, along with two others I didn't know at all. We decided, that night, to abscond several miles through the black-clotted skies to visit another friend. Long story short, he wasn't home and we re-routed back home. While we weren't near *Hell's Half Acre*, we did travel by dirt road sometimes stalking through ditches passing by large plots of farmland with decrepit barns – slats of wood splintered into chewed up remains – and formidable silos with stacks of bricks stretched up to towering heights. This set the stage for what would be the atmosphere of this story. Some other peculiar things happened that evening, but I don't think I'll get into it because it just might make its way into one of my next stories. I just love the setting of isolation out in the sticks. My hope is that you do too.

IT'S BEAUTIFUL ISN'T IT

Again, in my Nods, I spoke a little about the birth of this story. The only thing I'd like to stress is the topic of cochlear implants is a divisive one, and one I don't mean to drive a wedge into on purpose. There are schools of thought that debate for/against the cochlear implant, and I don't side with one over the other. The deaf community is a proud one and do not need sympathy because they have improved senses in other aspects. So, if you end up meeting a deaf/hard-of-hearing person, please don't feel the need to apologize for their deafness, and please don't call them hearing impaired. They want to be treated the same as everyone else.

Also, this is one whole story. In my initial release, there was confusion about the 'collection of poetry in the middle'. This time, I've numbered the sections just to curb the confusion and added an extra note here!

MEAT HOOK MAMBO

Meat Hook Mambo is what you get when you post a challenge on Facebook and take your friends to task on writing the most macabre obituary/eventful death they can conjure. The one with the most gruesome, convincing circumstance would be turned into a short story. Turns out, only three people decided to respond, but they also happened to be real-life friends instead of the virtual kind who stalk your posts and wait for you to say something political so they can disagree. I liked them all so much that I decided they all could be a part of the story.

Jam, Sam, and Zoe are to thank for this bit of horror noir I concocted. They gave me Ram Jam the Clown, the tipsy rescue lady, and the hunk of torso hoisted on a meat hook. From there, I let my fingers clack away on the keyboard and came up with Ham Seller and Cline Towers from the fictional wasteland and I couldn't be any happier with the results. Cheers!

PLIGHT OF THE PITIFUL

This one came in a nightmare as well, but the circumstances weren't nearly what this came out to be. Really, the only similarity between what I dreamt that night and this story is that it was set in a trailer park. That's all.

My imagination placed a panic-stricken me running from trailer to trailer, and around the trailer blocks as a song played on loop over what sounded like a phonograph that appeared to travel with me everywhere I went while a murderer was afoot.

Flea was such a dear character to me. I felt every wrong done to him and was in terrible shape when his fate was decided. A part of me died when he passed. That's the thing about this writing business that every writer will tell you. I'm sure at some point, each character will desensitize you in their own way and eventually the calloused edges will protect me from the emotional attachment, but I hope that isn't the case.

Truth be told, this was the hardest and most rewarding story to write. It took me to dark places, made me feel hope, and devastated me when I realized what had to be done to close the chapter to this story. And the book for that matter.

That's that. I hope you enjoyed my short stories. If you feel so inclined, please take a moment and wander over to Amazon or Goodreads (or scream into the sky) and tell me if you loved or hated it.

C. J. Bow is a very amateur writer with a hint of skill. He has written this book and this book alone. He's trying guys. Take it easy on him. He's sensitive.

Once invited to your home, or group chat, he'll ask obnoxious questions like, 'Where do we put the coats?" knowing full well that there is no virtual closet nor an imaginary bed to lay your parka or peacoat.

Please keep his wife and daughter in your thoughts while they put up with his relentless antics. They thank you in advance.

Twitter: @c_j_bow

Instagram: @cjb0w

Made in the USA
Monee, IL
05 April 2021

64873798R00113